PENGUIN BOOKS

BRITISH SHORT STORIES OF TODAY

British Short Stories of Today

Edited by Esmor Jones

PENGUIN BOOKS

Penguin Books Ltd, Harmondsworth, Middlesex, England
Viking Penguin Inc., 40 West 23rd Street, New York, New York 10010, U.S.A.
Penguin Books Australia Ltd, Ringwood, Victoria, Australia
Penguin Books Canada Ltd, 2801 John Street, Markham, Ontario, Canada L3R 1B4
Penguin Books (N.Z.) Ltd, 182–190 Wairau Road, Auckland 10, New Zealand

First published 1987

Typeset, printed and bound in Great Britain by
Hazell Watson & Viney Limited,
Member of the BPCC Group,
Aylesbury, Bucks
Typeset in Linotron Plantin

Contents

Introduction

The short stories in this collection have mostly been written very recently – a few in 1985. They have all been previously published, however, in collections or in magazines. The authors themselves come from all over Great Britain – northern and southern England, Scotland and Wales. Many are professional writers with much published work to their credit. A few are amateurs, in the best sense, with writing as an enthralling hobby. Others are at the beginning, they hope, of a life in writing.

If the authors are a mixed bunch, so are the stories. Whether serious or sad, suspenseful or comic, set in the past, present or future, these stories all offer, as short stories must, insights into character. We see how people react to situations or happenings; and the people are of all ages and backgrounds. Occasionally the central figure is not human at all – see Arthur C. Clarke's warning tale 'The Curse', where the 'character' is a river, perhaps England itself.

Not so long ago, it was often said that the short story was a dying art. Well, here is plenty of evidence to the contrary. The short story is alive and very well!

ESMOR JONES

The Poets and the Housewife

A FABLE

Martin Armstrong

Martin Armstrong died in 1974 at the age of ninety-two. He wrote both novels and histories, but is, perhaps, best known for his short stories.

'The Poets and the Housewife' makes use of an old way of telling stories to make very much a modern point. Appearances do deceive! So does the language. It looks like old English (it is a fable) but there are surprises.

The story was written before Britain adopted a decimal currency. Roughly, a shilling is five pence.

Once upon a time, on a summer's day, two poets, having shut up shop, went out into the country to collect copy, for their stock of this commodity was exhausted.

And they were careful to dress themselves carelessly: one put on a black collar and black-and-white checked trousers, and the other a cravat of raging scarlet, 'for' they thought (though they did not say so) 'we must dress the part'. And their hats were wide and reckless and the hair beneath their hats was like the thatch upon a broad-eaved barn.

And as they journeyed, poking about with their walking sticks after the precious substance of their quest, there gathered over their heads the devil of a storm.

And at the proper moment the storm burst and the rain came down and the poets left off seeking for copy and huddled under a hawthorn tree. And they appeared as two proud exotic birds, lighted down from the Lord knows where.

And there was a lodge near the hawthorn tree, and the lodge-keeper's wife looked out and, seeing the two, she exclaimed: 'Lord, look what the wet brings out!' And the rain increased fearfully.

And after a while she looked out again and the poets were changed, for their bloom was impaired, the rain had clotted their hair, and the scarlet cravat of the one had become crimson from saturation. And rain dripped from all their extremities.

And the lodgekeeper's wife was grieved for them and called out: 'Young men, will you not come in? Why play the heron who stands lugubrious with his feet in cold water when it is open to you to become as sparrows twittering with gladness beneath the eaves?'

But they bowed politely and replied: 'Thanks awfully, ma'am, but we are poets and we like it.'

And the lodgekeeper's wife was riled and sneered at them, remarking: 'They have certainly had a drop too much.' But they, smiling deprecatingly upon her, responded: 'Madam you are pleased to be dry.' 'And you,' quoth she, 'are pleased to be wet.' And she slammed-to the window, casting up her eyes and inquiring rhetorically, 'Did you ever?' and 'What next?'

And the rain came down like hell, leaping a foot high and sousing all things.

And after another while, the lodgekeeper's wife looked out again, and the two had gathered closer about the trunk of the hawthorn-tree, and they were as two old crows, for their shoulders were up and their beaks were down and they were unbelievably dishevelled.

And she shouted to them again, for she was a charitable woman, saying: 'O miserable gentlemen, in the name of civilization and commonsense, come inside.'

But they dared not turn their faces to her, lest the water should run down their necks: so, revolving themselves all of a piece, they replied: 'Renewed thanks, ma'am, but we are very well, for we are acquiring copy.' And they cowered under the deluge with great earnestness of purpose.

But the lodgekeeper's wife did not understand the word *copy*, so that she was amazed beyond measure and the power of comment was taken from her.

And the storm, having stormed itself out, abated: and the place was bathed in delicious smells of breathing leaves, and the warm sweetness of hawthorn perfumed the air.

Andd the lodgekeeper's wife looked out from the window a fourth and last time, and the poets were in the act of departure. And the tragedy of their appearance was beyond all comparing. For the scarlet of the cravat of one had run down into the bosom of his shirt, so that he was, as it were, a robin-redbreast. And both were soaked to the uttermost.

And when those poets were returned home, the one found that he had lost a shirt and the other that he had gained a cold. Therefore the one went out and bought a new shirt at seven and six and dear at that, and the other got himself a shilling bottle of Ammoniated Quinine which was tolerably cheap considering.

And the one wrote an ode called *Midsummer Storm* for which he obtained five guineas, so that (deducting fourpence for stamps and seven and six for the shirt) his net profit was four pounds seventeen and twopence.

But the other could only manage a one-guinea sonnet called *Rain Among Leaves*, so that (deducting fourpence for stamps and a shilling for the quinine) his net profit was nineteen and eightpence.

Thus the two acquired great store of copy (more, indeed, than they bargained for) and the sum of five pounds sixteen shillings and tenpence thrown in.

But the wife of the lodgekeeper knew nothing of all this, so that she still believes, like many another ill-informed person, that poets are nothing more than unpractical dreamers.

Ammoniated Quinine: an old-fashioned remedy for colds and fevers
guinea: in old money one pound and one shilling. It used to be a gold coin. In other words, £1.05p not allowing for inflation! There were twelve pence in a shilling and twenty shillings in a pound

Dingo

F. Bennett

This is a tale of the Australian outback – that is, the ranching country inland from the cities. 'Dingo' is written from experience. F. Bennett is English and lives in Hastings, but spent many years working with sheep and cattle on Australian ranches or 'stations'. It is a lonely life and it has a language of its own.

From all the dogs roaming the world, unwanted, unloved, I had to give my affection to a half-bred dingo, the wild dog of the Australian outback. This bitch that became mine, gradually digging her way into my heart with her natural skill and loving ways, was no beauty, except in my eyes. She was lop-eared, long-legged, her fur hard, yellow from her dingo and kelpie forebears, this last breed being the sheep dog reared on so many sheep stations for their working strain. Her golden eyes were her one redeeming feature; their shining depth showed a fine intelligence. As a pup she displayed no sign of the killer instinct of the dingo, the reason they are hated, hunted, trapped and poisoned on the big cattle and sheep stations. One dingo will, in a night, wound many sheep in its desperate chase through a herd, seeking a victim; or a pack of those wild dogs will hunt down a cow with a new-born calf, separate them from a mob of cattle, and worry the weakened cow until they can part her from her offspring, when they rush in for the kill. Call a man a dingo down under and he'll feel wounded for life; it's considered the most deadly insult.

Boundary riding in the Georgina country, bordering the Northern Territory, the far north-west cattle country of Australia, I came upon this pup. Mine was a lonely job but a good one, that is if you find enjoyment in the wide open spaces of outback Aussie, which I did. I got to know and love every tree: the Coolibar, Gum, Box, even the vast, dry, empty paddocks and acres of Spinnifex; tufts of thorny growth that seem to exist without water, for it was drought country, often missed by the yearly monsoonal rains. Flowers would not survive the scorching heat of those vast plains, but flocks of birds, budgerigars, green in undulating flight, huge white cockatoos, vivid parrots, gave colour and life as they flew around or rested like gorgeous blooms on the trees.

Happily I rode the paddocks, repairing broken fences; reporting to the station manager movement of cattle; herding small mobs back to the paddock from whence they had strayed. They say a cow or bull will go through any fence, if it has a mind to do so, and I have often seen them skilfully easing their way through the fencing, built as it is outback with stout posts run through with several rows of wiring.

I carried my tucker in the saddle bag, bread, meat, tea, and at noon, after a hard morning's riding, boiled my quart pot over a bushman's fire, a few dry leaves and twigs, soon ignited, enjoying a brief respite from the blazing heat around me.

My home was a hut, not too badly furnished with all the necessities for living, situated ten miles from the station homestead, from whence I rode out six days a week, happy in the freedom of my life, the continual blue skies, the peacefulness of it all.

I'd settled down to enjoy my break, a quick meal and brief shut-eye, when I spotted this pup. There was movement amongst some nearby lignum bushes, and a small bundle of fur, all yellow, golden eyes, came waggling through the bush. Apart from birds and cattle, animal life in that vast countryside was rare; a stray 'roo, a rabbit or so was all you would expect to see, and in the heat of high noon nothing ever stirs in the stillness and silence of outback Australia. I called her to me and after a while she came and let me stroke her. I fed her cooled tea, diluted from a nearby billabong, which seemed to go down a treat. She might have been abandoned by Abos gone walkabout; there were signs of a deserted camp, bag humpy and bower shed, old bones and the leavings of a big camp fire. 'You're lucky,' I told her, 'you wouldn't have survived long in this heat.'

So Lucky she became. I propped her upon the pommel of my saddle, steadied my bay gelding while I mounted, and rode for home. It was Saturday, the heat was past bearing.

'roo: kangaroo *billabong*: branch of a river or pool
Abos gone walkabout: this refers to the custom of Aborigine boys going out alone into the wild for a period to mark their becoming men
bag humpy: a rough temporary hut of the kind the Aborigines build

I became the devoted slave of my Lucky; I lavished upon her round yellow body all the love of a lonely man, and watched her grow from a hard ball of fur to a lean young bitch. I loved the look of her: golden eyes, slim muscular body, white-tipped tail, held erect like a pennant in movement.

Early morning, when I rode out on the night horse to round up my small string of working horses, yarding them to select my mount for the day, she would run beside me, leaping high, somersaulting with the sheer joy of living; and when it was necessary to check a straying animal she was there, young as she was, heeling them, wheeling them; she was all a cattle dog should be, which was strange considering her lineage, but that's the way it turns out sometimes.

She was always by my side when I rode out on my inspection of the fences, and when she became tired, being not yet fully grown, I would mount her on the pommel, and we rode together in close, happy companionship. My horse made no objection; a boundary rider's horses are dependable animals, quiet, steady, sometimes half-draft; a frisky mount, liable to pull away, is the last thing you need, riding the outback fences.

I fed her the best, plenty of raw meat and big bones. Daily, with small tweezers, I removed from her body, the corners of those golden eyes, deep inside her ears, the ghastly ticks that plague station dogs; little spider-like creatures fat with blood, that cling to and feed on certain animals. It was a nauseating job, grabbing them and pulling them free, killing them, but I was dead sure my Lucky would not be plagued by them. She repaid me with her devotion; my shadow by day, sleeping beside me at night. Hurt beyond measure if I ever reprimanded her, her golden eyes would regard me with unbelieving sorrow as she cringed to the ground, bewildered and tortured by the absence of my usual affection.

She was only ten months old when the boss drove out early one morning to my hut. This was unusual, he always contacted me by the station phone every evening after I'd returned from my daily round of inspecting and repairing. Perhaps the lines were down; there'd been a quick, scurrying storm the previous evening, fierce winds, thunder to rock you backwards, early monsoonal rain, heavy, hurtling straight down from the heavens. Lucky had been a

down under: English term for Australia. Look at a globe to see why!
outback: country beyond the populated coastal areas

little scared and sheltered under the kitchen table; now she growled at this intruder as he stood framed in the doorway.

The boss eyed my pet with distaste as we chatted for a few minutes about the work in hand and then 'get those cleanskins in Adelaide paddock,' he instructed me, 'and drown that flaming dingo.' Aussies are like that, especially in the great outback; downright, forthright. Station life is hard, serious, there's no time for mucking about. If the boss gives an order it is carried out at once.

I should have known my dingo pup would never be tolerated on that cattle station; I had known and had ignored the inevitable issue; now I had to face and come to grips with the result of my foolishness.

As I saddled up and prepared for my ride, hurt and irresolute, I found my eyes continually straying to my beloved Lucky as she sat before me, erect, eyes on mine. With the infallible sixth sense that animals of all species possess, she knew, she was waiting for my verdict.

Of course I couldn't do it; I could no more hurt her, drown her, shoot her, than jump off Sydney Bridge; my whole recent life had been geared to her care and protection. She was everything to me and a great help too in my daily work. The boss, I told myself, was being very unreasonable. I climbed slowly into the saddle and rode for Adelaide paddock. Lucky ran beside me, leaping, somersaulting, coming to heel when I whistled.

The cleanskins grazed happily in Adelaide paddock; I approached them cautiously, Lucky at heel; one false move and they'd be gone with the wind. It had been a long hard ride, an early start and now, at full noon, the sun blazed, scorching down. After the big muster, these were the ones missed, unbranded; they had to be rounded up, brought into the stockyard for branding.

I was excited, elated; in that vast country you were not always lucky enough to ride upon them. I cantered towards them, cows, calves, young steers; they bellowed at my approach, left their grazing and moved onwards.

I had them on the go, cantering I moved them homewards. I looked for Lucky, couldn't see her; she was still a pup, it had been a long hard grind, I was expecting too much from her. My work must come first; it was exhilarating, rewarding to be herding home those cleanskins.

cleanskins: cattle not yet branded with the brand of the station

But continually my eyes searched the far paddocks as I wheeled and herded the stragglers; I looked for movement, any sign of my pup. Now that the herd was on the go I'd have galloped to her, let her ride on the pommel as so often before.

The paddock was starkly bare, just browned acres of grassland, no bush or tree to hide her from me. My Lucky never returned. When I'd yarded the cleanskins, I rode out to find her, searching the paddocks, longing for a sight of her. I searched until the sudden southern night wiped away all light; she was not to be found; she was half dingo; I could only hope that her natural savage inheritance of self-preservation would protect her. I felt weakened by my physical effort and drained of all life's meaning. Sadly I rode the trail to my lonely hut.

Life went on; station work is demanding, the constant care of animals, fences, equipment. My days were busy; it was the long nights when I felt so lost, lonely, hurt by the absence of my beloved pup. I missed her so much it was torture sitting there, trying to read by my carbide light. I'd find jobs, mend things, but the hours to bedtime were still so long, so empty. Station dogs are always housed in the home paddock adjacent to the night horse or the big garages; their life is severe, forever chained, small kennels, meagre food; they are bred to work, this being the only time they are unleashed and allowed to run. My Lucky had broken all rules, enjoying the home comforts of my hut, sharing my life; she'd been my constant shadow; I missed her at every turn.

I was trailing the station milkers, a small mob of Jerseys and Friesians. For reasons of their own they'd gone through the home paddock fences and I'd been sent to find them.

They'd gone through all fences, I found, heading for that vast wilderness of far west Australia. I tracked them, not easy in that drought country, and after a hard ride had come upon them, still heading westwards.

Being domestic animals they were easy to handle and at sight of me they turned and headed for home. I was fond of them, big lumbering cows, gentle as babies; I knew them all by name and was urging them onwards when I became aware of the yellow shadows skulking behind the stragglers; a pack of dingos who looked lean and hungry enough to attack; there would be little food for them in that bare country.

At a distance they circled now; this was something I'd never experienced before, although I knew the savagery of those wild dogs when hungry. They were circling the herd and me, awaiting the right moment for attack, the cows leaping, bucking and bellowing in fear.

And then I saw my Lucky, leaner, full grown, she ran with the mob, snarling! So she'd gone to the pack! I'd thought so, guessed this must be the reason for her disappearance; I'd known that if she'd wanted to, she'd have found her way back to me.

I whistled fiercely, the old whistle she'd known so well, piercing, commanding her to come to me. I fell from my saddle, embracing her as she leapt into my arms, licking my face, jumping high, somersaulting to show her joy at our meeting.

I fondled her, whispering words of endearment; tears came to my eyes as I felt the warmth of her yellow fur and saw once again the golden gleam of her beautiful eyes. Now I'd never let her go.

The dogs had fallen back a bit, still circling. I clutched my long-lost pet to me, hugging her; Lucky moved restlessly, licking my face. I began to form vague plans in my mind, how to hold her, keep her from the pack. It was my responsibility to protect the milkers, to get them safely home, and yet I believe, in that great moment of joy and relief at finding my pet again, I would have abandoned the cows for the love of that bitch.

A big Jersey bellowed high in fear, kicking at the yellow shape that snapped at her heels.

Then the hard ground was echoing with the drumming of hooves; a mob of riders hurtled towards me, galloping hard, scattering dust tree high. They were my mates from the station, I could recognize them as they drew nearer; they were the stockmen and ringers with whom I rode at the annual muster; now, seeing the danger, they were riding to help me.

Alerted and scared by the thundering mob of horses, the dingos scattered in alarm, then, swerving into a tight pack, moving as one animal, following their leader, were off, racing away in a frightened bunch.

The horsemen galloped to my side; I looked for Lucky, whistled frantically as I saw her streaking to join the pack, her long slim body flat out, tail held high like a waving pennant. Soon she was up with the leader, heading for the never-never land of far west Australia.

The German Boy

Ron Butlin

How not to help a lonely child from another country! Klaus, the German boy of the title, was at an English boarding-school for boys. The English boys at the school came from prosperous homes, and there is a hint that this is another way in which Klaus differs. The story is full of hints; we guess why Klaus comes so much into the mind of the story-teller.

Ron Butlin lives and works in Edinburgh and has published two volumes of poetry as well as a collection of short stories.

The woman I can see standing outside in the pouring rain reminds me of Klaus, the German boy. It is the expression on her face: she looks . . . so desolate, so utterly unloved. People hurry past her as quickly as possible; if someone does smile, I watch her hesitate for a moment. Then she looks away.

When I came to the office about half-an-hour ago I passed her by pretending interest in a shop-display. From here, however, I can study her in perfect safety. Perhaps she is waiting for someone. I realize now that she could not have been taken in by my elaborate charade for it is repeated every few minutes by others – repeated too frequently to be convincing. At one time I might have pitied her, for that kind of cruelty comes easiest of all. Believe me, I know – Klaus taught me that.

This morning I have come to the office and done nothing. There is a pile of correspondence for me, some of it marked 'urgent'. Instead I stand and stare out of the window at the well-dressed woman opposite. She is in her mid-forties. I think she is crying but it is difficult to tell at this distance. She has glanced in my direction so I will move back from the window.

I remember my headmaster talking to us before Klaus was brought in.

'There is nothing special about him,' he said. 'Remember, he is just like the rest of us.'

When he came into the classroom for the first time, however, it was quite obvious he was not like the rest of us: Klaus looked different, he talked different and, even though he wore the same clothes as us, somehow he seemed to be dressed differently. Everyone looked at him and he looked at the floor. He had fair hair, very pale skin and was quite tall. His shoulders were trembling – an action his long arms increased proportionally, making his hands jerk as if they were receiving a series of small electric shocks.

'This is Klaus, he is going to join your class.' The headmaster was a small red-faced man who always looked as if he was too small and too red-faced to be comfortable. When he died a few months later from sunstroke I imagined him as having simply exploded one very hot afternoon.

My family talked a great deal about 'class' which for a long time I confused with my schoolfriends who were all of one class in both senses of the word. 'He is of a different class altogether' meant, to me, that someone was simply a few years older or younger than myself. And when my Aunt Claire happened to remark during an Open Day that Klaus was of a different class to the rest of the boys, I hastened to correct her saying that on the contrary he was the same age as myself and we sat next to each other and were the very best of friends. She said I was a very kind and thoughtful boy; and I replied excitedly that I was going to learn German. 'Of course you should help him to be at his ease, but you mustn't neglect your proper studies,' she concluded with a smile.

Klaus didn't even glance at the class he was about to join. He looked more uncomfortable than ever: his knees began shaking and his hands, in an effort to control the effects of the 'electric shocks', had grasped his jacket tightly at the sides – which served only to increase his nervous jerkings by the amount of 'give' in the material.

The headmaster ushered him to one side of a map of the world which had the British Empire coloured red, 'an unfortunate choice of colour' my aunt had observed during her visit. Then he indicated Germany and spoke to Klaus in German: he replied, '*Ja, mein Herr*' without raising his eyes from the floor. And then a moment later he did look up – not at the map, however, but at us; and he smiled, then blushed and returned his gaze to the floor. A boy sniggered. The headmaster plodded on.

'Klaus is from Germany. This is Germany.' He indicated it again. ' – *Deutschland*.' He smiled at Klaus then looked at us once more.

'*Deutschland* – that's "Germany" in German. Now, does anyone here speak German?' The boy who had sniggered before shouted out, '*Ja, mein Herr*' making us all laugh.

Klaus sat next to me. He didn't speak English but we managed somehow in Latin. He told me he had been born and brought up in Germany but when his father died his mother had married an Englishman. He had only been here a week but he liked it. He said that he and I were friends – *amici sumus*. That was nearly twenty years ago.

I really should get down to some work. Normally I work hard, very hard. In the name of Cochrane and Assocs., I deal in money: I buy it, sell it, lend it. I deal only with certain people and in private. They have confidence in me. They assume that having maintained credibility in the past, then our house will do so in the future – and perhaps they are right, for as long as they trust us then we can do business and so justify that trust. In the course of time I am expected to become head of the firm. I would have liked that.

When I was a child our family was well-off. There was an inheritance which my father employed wisely. I attended public school before going up to Oxford to read Classics. I was hard-working rather than brilliant. My father died when I was in my third year and I returned home immediately, to be told that he had committed suicide. We were completely bankrupt. Everything had to be sold; I had to leave Oxford and begin working in the City. For the last ten years I have worked hard to restore the family name.

Last night we had a special dinner, Sylvia and I, to celebrate our wedding anniversary – we have been married for five years. Afterwards she said she was proud of me as a husband, lover and merchant banker. She kissed me.

Recently I have had occasion to go over our company books and it has become apparent to me that our business methods are as hopelessly out-of-date as our furniture and fittings; and with our present commitments it is too late to correct the situation. We will be finished by the end of the year. Strictly speaking we are finished already but as yet no one else knows. However, once word gets around the City, we will have to shut-up shop: for a company that is failing, especially an old company, may inspire pity – but never investment. I want to tell my wife. I want to tell my partners.

Instead I say nothing. I stand at my office window staring out into the street at a complete stranger standing in the pouring rain. She has hardly moved from where I first saw her. She must be soaked through and very cold now. She appears very unhappy – I would like to go over and speak to her, to say 'Don't worry' or something like that; or perhaps even to smile at her from here. I would like to, but I know I won't.

On his first night in our dormitory Klaus was given the bed next to mine and I could hear him crying. The room was in darkness but I could just make him out under the blankets. He was kneeling and bending forwards with his head pushing into the pillow.

'Klaus, Klaus,' I called in a low voice. Quietly I went over to him and sat on his bed.

'Don't cry, don't cry. You're here now. It will be good – you and me together. Honest.'

He made some reply in a voice muffled as much by his tears as by the blankets. He probably hadn't understood a word I had said. I sat with him for nearly half-an-hour while he cried, then I went back to bed. The next night was the same, and every night afterwards. During the day he was fine: he worked hard in class and joined in the games. Gradually his English improved. Each night, however, he cried himself to sleep. Then one day, during the morning break, he told me that from then on he was going to speak only in German – except to me, of course. At first I thought he was joking, but he wasn't.

The next class was arithmetic and near the end of the lesson our teacher began going over the problems out loud.

'Klaus, No. 4 please, the one about the reservoir.' Klaus stood up to give his answer. He seemed uncertain and he mumbled. The teacher asked him to repeat it. He spoke more clearly this time: '*Zwei Minuten*.' The class laughed and even the teacher joined in a little before asking him to repeat it in English.

'*Zwei Minuten*.' The class laughed even louder, but this time the teacher didn't even smile.

'In English, Klaus, if you please,' he said quite firmly.

'*Zwei Minuten*,' Klaus repeated; his fingers were gripping the sides of the desk-lid and his body shook. The teacher asked him again, and again the class went into uproar at his reply. His face was white. He was gripping the desk so tightly it rattled against the floor. He began repeating his answer: '*Zwei Minuten Zwei Minuten Zwei Minuten* . . .' He was staring ahead, quite oblivious to the noise about him.

The teacher didn't know what to do . . . He told Klaus to sit down and he wouldn't. To be quiet and he wouldn't. To stand in the corner and he wouldn't. '*Zwei Minuten Zwei Minuten* . . .' Tears were running down his cheeks and his voice was choking but he couldn't stop. Finally he was taken to the sick-room.

He came back afterwards but still refused to speak English. A few days later he was sent home. I have never seen him since and hardly even given him a moment's thought until now.

It has stopped raining. The woman is still waiting there but in the sunlight, she looks less miserable. She has been there for forty minutes now, at least.

To work. I suppose I have to fill up the day somehow and then return home. And I will have to think how to tell Sylvia that the business is collapsing.

She will have cooked dinner for my arrival tonight and we will eat together with the children. Afterwards I will read them a bedtime story, then we will probably watch TV. A few hours later it will be time to go to bed – and still I will not have told her.

And tomorrow I will return to the office; and the day after. There will be letters marked 'urgent', cables, meetings, luncheons, delicate negotiations and so forth. And every evening I will return home to Sylvia. Back and forwards; back and forwards I will go saying nothing.

The woman has turned to check her appearance in the shop-window. She is adjusting her hat. I watch as she crosses the road and now walks quickly past my window and down the street.

I have sat down in my executive leather chair. At any moment the telephone may ring or my secretary announce someone to see me – until then I will do nothing except rest my feet on the desk. For how long? I wonder.

'*Zwei Minuten Zwei Minuten* . . .' I hear Klaus say – which I now understand as meaning a lifetime, or as good as.

Shopping for One

Anne Cassidy

Supermarkets are much the same the world over – especially the queues at check-out points. What extraordinary things other people are buying! There are odd snatches of overheard conversation too. But what if one is living alone, 'Shopping for One'?

'So what did you say?' Jean heard the blonde woman in front of her talking to her friend.

'Well,' the darker woman began, 'I said I'm not having that woman there. I don't see why I should. I mean I'm not being old-fashioned but I don't see why I should have to put up with her at family occasions. After all . . ..' Jean noticed the other woman giving an accompaniment of nods and headshaking at the appropriate parts. They fell into silence and the queue moved forward a couple of steps.

Jean felt her patience beginning to itch. Looking into her wire basket she counted ten items. That meant she couldn't go through the quick till but simply had to wait behind elephantine shopping loads; giant bottles of coke crammed in beside twenty-pound bags of potatoes and 'special offer' drums of bleach. Somewhere at the bottom, Jean thought, there was always a plastic carton of eggs or a see-through tray of tomatoes which fell casualty to the rest. There was nothing else for it – she'd just have to wait.

'After all,' the dark woman resumed her conversation, 'how would it look if she was there when I turned up?' Her friend shook her head slowly from side to side and ended with a quick nod.

Should she have got such a small size salad cream? Jean wasn't sure. She was sick of throwing away half-used bottles of stuff.

'He came back to you after all,' the blonde woman suddenly said. Jean looked up quickly and immediately felt her cheeks flush. She bent over and began to rearrange the items in her shopping basket.

'On his hands and knees,' the dark woman spoke in a triumphant voice. 'Begged me take him back.'

She gritted her teeth together. Should she go and change it for a larger size? Jean looked behind and saw that she was hemmed in by three large trollies. She'd lose her place in the queue. There was something so pitiful about buying small sizes of everything. It was as though everyone knew.

'You can always tell a person by their shopping,' was one of her mother's favourite maxims. She looked into her shopping basket: individual fruit pies, small salad cream, yoghurt, tomatoes, cat food and a chicken quarter.

'It was only for sex you know. He admitted as much to me when he came back,' the dark woman informed her friend. Her friend began to load her shopping on to the conveyor belt. The cashier, doing what looked like an in-depth study of a biro, suddenly said, 'Make it out to J. Sainsbury PLC.' She was addressing a man who had been poised and waiting to write out a cheque for a few moments. His wife was loading what looked like a gross of fish fingers into a cardboard box marked 'Whiskas'. It was called a division of labour.

Jean looked again at her basket and began to feel the familiar feeling of regret that visited her from time to time. Hemmed in between family-size cartons of cornflakes and giant packets of washing-powder, her individual yoghurt seemed to say it all. She looked up towards a plastic bookstand which stood beside the till. A slim glossy hardback caught her eye. The words *Cooking for One* screamed out from the front cover. Think of all the oriental foods you can get into, her friend had said. He was so traditional after all. Nodding in agreement with her thoughts Jean found herself eye to eye with the blonde woman, who, obviously not prepared to tolerate nodding at anyone else, gave her a blank, hard look and handed her what looked like a black plastic ruler with the words 'Next customer please' printed on it in bold letters. She turned back to her friend. Jean put the ruler down on the conveyor belt.

She thought about their shopping trips, before, when they were together, which for some reason seemed to assume massive proportions considering there were only two of them. All that rushing round, he pushing the trolley dejectedly, she firing questions at him. Salmon? Toilet rolls? Coffee? Peas? She remembered he only liked the processed kind. It was all such a performance. Standing there holding her wire basket, embarrassed by its very emptiness, was like something out of a soap opera.

'Of course, we've had our ups and downs,' the dark woman continued, lazily passing a few items down to her friend who was now on to what looked like her fourth Marks and Spencer carrier bag.

Jean began to load her food on to the conveyor belt. She picked up the cookery book and felt the frustrations of indecision. It was only ninety pence but it seemed to define everything, to pinpoint her aloneness, to prescribe an empty future. She put it back in its place.

'So that's why I couldn't have her there you see,' the dark woman was summing up. She lowered her voice to a loud whisper which immediately alerted a larger audience. 'And anyway, when he settles back in, I'm sure we'll sort out the other business then.' The friends exchanged knowing expressions and the blonde woman got her purse out of a neat leather bag. She peeled off three ten pound notes and handed them to the cashier.

Jean opened her carrier bag ready for her shopping. She turned to watch the two women as they walked off, the blonde pushing the trolley and the other seemingly carrying on with her story.

The cashier was looking expectantly at her and Jean realized that she had totalled up. It was four pounds and eighty-seven pence. She had the right money, it just meant sorting her change out. She had an inclination that the people behind her were becoming impatient. She noticed their stack of items all lined and waiting, it seemed, for starters orders. Brown bread and peppers, olive oil and lentils and, in the centre, a stray packet of beefburgers.

She gave over her money and picked up her carrier bag. She felt a sense of relief to be away from the mass of people. She felt out of place, a non conformer, half a consumer unit.

Walking out of the door she wondered what she might have for tea. Possibly chicken, she thought, with salad. Walking towards her car she thought that she should have bought the cookery book after all. She suddenly felt much better in the fresh air. She'd buy it next week. And in future she'd buy a large salad cream. After all, what if people came round unexpectedly?

The Curse

Arthur C. Clarke

Arthur C. Clarke is perhaps the most famous living British author of science fiction. He wrote the script for *2001: A Space Odyssey*. His stories often seem to have an uncanny knack of prophecy; we might pray it is not true of this one – though the world seems to live on.

For three hundred years, while its fame spread across the world, the little town had stood here at the river's bend. Time and change had touched it lightly; it had heard from afar both the coming of the Armada and the fall of the Third Reich, and all Man's wars had passed it by.

Now it was gone, as though it had never been. In a moment of time the toil and treasure of centuries had been swept away. The vanished streets could still be traced as faint marks in the vitrified ground, but of the houses, nothing remained. Steel and concrete, plaster and ancient oak – it had mattered little at the end. In the moment of death they had stood together, transfixed by the glare of the detonating bomb. Then, even before they could flash into fire, the blast waves had reached them and they had ceased to be. Mile upon mile the ravening hemisphere of flame had expanded over the level farmlands, and from its heart had risen the twisting totempole that had haunted the minds of men for so long, and to such little purpose.

The rocket had been a stray, one of the last ever to be fired. It was hard to say for what target it had been intended. Certainly not London, for London was no longer a military objective. London, indeed, was no longer anything at all. Long ago the men whose duty it was had calculated that three of the hydrogen bombs would be sufficient for that rather small target. In sending twenty, they had been perhaps a little over-zealous.

This was not one of the twenty that had done their work so well.

Both its destination and its origin were unknown: whether it had come across the lonely Arctic wastes or far above the waters of the Atlantic, no one could tell and there were few now who cared. Once there had been men who had known such things, who had watched from afar the flight of the great projectiles and had sent their own missiles to meet them. Often that appointment had been kept, high above the Earth where the sky was black and sun and stars shared the heavens together. Then there had bloomed for a moment that indescribable flame, sending out into space a message that in centuries to come other eyes than Man's would see and understand.

But that had been days ago, at the beginning of the War. The defenders had long since been brushed aside, as they had known they must be. They had held on to life long enough to discharge their duty; too late, the enemy had learned his mistake. He would launch no further rockets; those still falling he had dispatched hours ago on secret trajectories that had taken them far out into space. They were returning now unguided and inert, waiting in vain for the signals that should lead them to their destinies. One by one they were falling at random upon a world which they could harm no more.

The river had already overflowed its banks; somewhere down its course the land had twisted beneath that colossal hammer-blow and the way to the sea was no longer open. Dust was still falling in a fine rain, as it would do for days as Man's cities and treasures returned to the world that had given them birth. But the sky was no longer wholly darkened, and in the west the sun was settling through banks of angry cloud.

A church had stood here by the river's edge, and though no trace of the building remained, the gravestones that the years had gathered round it still marked its place. Now the stone slabs lay in parallel rows, snapped off at their bases and pointing mutely along the line of the blast. Some were half flattened into the ground, others had been cracked and blistered by terrific heat, but many still bore the messages they had carried down the centuries in vain.

The light died in the west and the unnatural crimson faded from the sky. Yet still the graven words could be clearly read, lit by a steady, unwavering radiance, too faint to be seen by day but strong enough to banish night. The land was burning: for miles the glow of its radioactivity was reflected from the clouds. Through the glimmering landscape wound the dark ribbon of the steadily widening river, and as the waters submerged the land that deadly glow continued unchanging in the depths. In a generation, perhaps, it would have faded from sight, but a hundred years might pass before life would safely come this way again.

Timidly the waters touched the worn gravestone that for more than three hundred years had laid before the vanished altar. The church that had sheltered it so long had given it some protection at the last, and only a slight discolouration of the rock told of the fires that had passed this way. In the corpse-light of the dying land, the archaic words could still be traced as the water rose around them, breaking at last in tiny ripples across the stone. Line by line the epitaph upon which so many millions had gazed slipped beneath the conquering waters. For a little while the letters could still be faintly seen; then they were gone forever.

Good frend for Iesvs sake forbeare,
To digg the dvst encloased heare
Blest be ye man yt spares thes stones,
And cvrst be he yt moves my bones.

Undisturbed through all eternity the poet could sleep in safety now: in the silence and darkness above his head, the Avon was seeking its new outlet to the sea.

The epitaph is hundreds of years old. In modernized spelling:

Good friend for Jesus' sake forbear,
To dig the dust enclosèd here.
Blest be the man that spares these stones,
And cursed be he that moves my bones.

The Avon is an English river; you may have heard of Shakespeare's birthplace: Stratford on Avon. Avon is actually from a Welsh word meaning river.

The Time Keeper

Elspeth Davie

'The man is clock-mad.' Well, that's the verdict of the young on Renwick the lawyer who shows people round Edinburgh. But what makes him tick?

Elspeth Davie was born and educated in Edinburgh. She is married with one daughter. She has published three novels and three collections of short stories.

It was taken as a matter of course that at one time or other during the summer he would be showing people around his city. Renwick was a hospitable man and for certain weeks it was a duty to be available to visitors. The beauty of the place was written on its skyline in a sharp, black script of spires, chimneys and turrets and in the flowing line of a long crag and hill. It was written up in books. He had shelves devoted to its history and its architecture. It was written on anti-litter slogans with the stern injunction that this was a beautiful city and it had better be kept that way.

Sometimes the people he took on were those wished on him for an hour or two, friends of friends, or persons he'd met by chance passing through on their way north. They were all sightseers of a sort and the first sight they wanted to see, particularly if they were foreigners, was himself. Well, he was on the spot of course. Yes, he had to admit he probably *was* a sight and even worth looking at in a very superficial way. At certain times he put on his advocate's garb – a highly stylized get-up, dark, narrow and formal. A bowler hat went with the suit and an umbrella which – because of the windiness of the city – often remained unrolled. He was never solemn about the business. He was the first to point out that it was traditional wear – a kind of fancy dress or disguise. 'And there are plenty of them about these days,' he would say. 'We ourselves are falling behind in the game. Look at all the people either dressing the part or the opposite of the part!' But there was no need of excuse.

Visitors enjoyed him in his dress and were disappointed to discover he seldom wore it when the Court was not sitting. Sometimes however they were lucky. And he had a face that went with the garb – a rather masked face, long and grave with hair well plastered down over a neat skull as though to show what an extreme of flatness could be achieved in comparison with the dashing wig which he might later put on.

Renwick's hospitality didn't mean that he was always a patient man. There was a good deal of exasperation and sharpness in his character, and he shared with many of his fellow citizens a highly argumentative and sceptical turn of mind. He developed it and was valued for it. That hint of the suspicious Scot in his make-up was well hidden. The impatience was not so well in check. It boiled up silently at dullness. It occasionally exploded at stupidity. As time went on he had even begun to be impatient with those visitors who insisted on taking a purely romantic view of the city. It was not, after all, made up only of interesting stones, nor were the people going about their business on top of these stones particularly romantic. Certainly not. They were a common-sense, very businesslike lot and more to be compared to down-to-earth scene-shifters doing their jobs against a theatrical background.

This was made clear to an American couple one afternoon as they stood with him in one of the oldest graveyards of the city. There was a great deal to see and a lot to hear about. Renwick had given them something of the turbulent history of the place and listed the succession of famous persons who had been buried here. They in their turn exclaimed about the ancient monuments and walls. They touched the moss-covered dates on headstones. It was getting late. The three or four still left in the place were slowly making their way out. In the distance a blonde girl was moving round the dark church between black and white tombstones. But Renwick's couple were all for lingering in the place until the sun went down. Renwick felt a sudden flare of impatience rise inside him. He directed them to look up and out of the place. From where they stood they could see, rising on all sides, the backs of houses and churches, and beyond that a glimpse of the bridge which carried a busy street over a chasm. Cars and buses crossed it. People went striding past. 'But look up there,' he said pointing. 'We are rather an energetic crowd. You can see we're in a hurry. You're not going to find your ordinary citizen of the place sitting around staring at old stones for long. I believe you might find it hard enough to get him to stop and talk for any length of time unless there was very good reason for it. For better or worse – that is our character!'

The Americans didn't deny this. They had already attempted to detain people on the bridge. They had sensed the bracing air. Now, polite but silent, they stared down at an angel whose round and rather sulky face was crowned by a neat, green crewcut of moss and backed by frilly wings sprouting behind his ears. Cautiously they mentioned the old ghosts of the place. 'But just behind you,' came the brisk voice, 'there in that wall, there are still lived-in houses. Look at that window for instance.' It was true that in the actual ancient wall of the place they were looking into the room of a house. Sitting in the open window was an old man being shaved by someone standing behind. At first they saw only a hand holding his chin, the other hand drawing a razor along his cheek. But while they watched the job was done. The head of the old man and his middle-aged daughter emerged from the window. It was close enough to get a clear sight of them – keen, unsmiling, both staring down with eyes which were shrewd but without much curiosity, as though they had seen decades of tourists standing just below them there on that particular spot in the churchyard.

'You see there are more than just angels around us,' said Renwick tersely. 'There are also ordinary, busy folk getting on with their own jobs.' The young couple looked for a moment as though they might question the busyness and even the ordinariness, but had thought better of it, especially as they had seen Renwick look openly at his wrist.

Renwick counted himself a polite man. Lately, however, he had given in to this habit, common to persons of consequence in the city, of glancing at his watch – and often while people were actually talking to him. He believed that he was indicating in the politest possible way that he was a very busy man, that even in summer his time was limited. But as the habit grew not only visitors but even friends began to see the wrist shoot out, no longer surreptitiously but very openly. Those who still hung around after that had only themselves to blame. And as well as the watch he was very well up in the tactics of the engagement diary. 'Well, certainly not tomorrow, nor the day after. This week's out in fact. Next week? Full up,

I'm afraid. No, I have a space here. I think I can *just* about manage to fit you in.' Acquaintances might sound grateful but they felt squeezed and sometimes throttled as they watched him writing them into the minimal space between appointments.

Just as Renwick was proud and yet irritated by the romantic reputation of the city, so he felt about the supernatural history of the place. He was good-natured about disguises, masks of all kinds. He understood the hidden. But the guise of the supernatural he didn't care for. He had lost count of the number of times he was asked about the witches and warlocks of the city, medieval apparitions hidden down closes, the eighteenth-century ghosts of the New Town. Grudgingly he pointed to deserted windows where heads had looked out and stairs where persons without their heads had walked down. Reluctantly he led willing visitors to the district where the major had made his pact, pointed out infamous tenements and doorways blasted with the Devil's curse. 'And now you'll want to see the spot where the gallows stood – and you'll not mind if I leave you there. I have to keep an eye on my time. The fact is I have a good deal of business to attend to between now and supper.'

Friends dated his concern with time back to a year when his post brought new responsibilities. Others pointed out that busyness was all a matter of choice and that the time-obsession was common to most middle-aged men once they'd begun to feel it making up on them. 'And worse things can happen to a man than working to a tight schedule,' remarked a colleague as they discussed others in the profession. 'We've had a good few suicides by his age, and quite a tearing of the silk. There was McInnes letting it all rip and making off for the South Seas. And Webster? Wasn't it the stage he'd always yearned for, never the Bar? Yes, retired now, white hair to the shoulders – happy enough they say, and no guile in the man at all. Still, meeting him late on summer nights in loopy hats with orange feathers gave some people more of a turn than seeing the Devil himself.' Other names came up. They decided if it was nothing more than a little touchiness about time – Renwick was doing well enough.

By midsummer a stream of holiday-makers were on the streets. Renwick would become impatient – or was it envious? – at the idea of an endless enjoyment of leisure. How could they wander for days and weeks, sometimes for months? From early spring when the first few aimless visitors arrived he would begin to take note of the city clocks. Not that he hadn't known them all his life – the clocks under church spires, the clocks on schools and hospitals and church towers. He'd seen brand-new timepieces erected in his day and had attended the unveilings of memorial clocks. But now he counted them as allies in the summer game, to give him backing when the wristwatch methods had no result. It was his habit, then, to stare about him for the nearest clock – if it was old so much the better. Having alerted visitors to its history it was an easy step to exclaim at the time of day, to excuse himself and make off at all possible speed to the next appointment.

During one summer Renwick had several visitors of his own for a short time. He enjoyed their stay. They knew the city well. It was not always necessary to accompany them, but he had the pleasure of their talk in the evening. Later, however, he was asked if he would help a friend out with four visitors who had been staying in the city and, with little warning, were to land on him for twelve hours. The friend had to be out of town on the evening of that day. Could Renwick possibly take them round for half an hour or so? Yes, he could do that. When the time came they turned out to be two middle-aged couples from the south who had not set foot in the city before this visit. But they had read the necessary books. They were well primed with history and they knew legends about every door and windowframe. They had expected smoky sunsets and they got them. They knew that on certain nights there might be a moon directly above the floodlit castle. The moon was in the prescribed spot the first night they'd arrived. They did not mind bad weather. They said that gloom and darkness suited the place. They liked the mist and even the chill haar that could swirl up out of the sea after a warm day. They were amiable and they had an equal and unqualified love for all the figures in the city's past.

That evening Renwick had taken them down into one of the closes of the Lawnmarket and they were now standing in a large court enclosed by tenement walls. There were a few people besides themselves in the place – a group of youths with bottles bulging at their hips, a fair-haired girl holding a guidebook and three small children who had rushed in after a ball and out again. It was getting late and a few small yellow lights were showing high up on the surrounding walls.

haar: a sea-mist; a cold, damp fog

'If only we could get in and see some of those weird old rooms,' said one of the wives, staring up.

'And speak to one or two of the old folk,' her husband added. 'There'll be ones up there with many a tale to tell of the old days.'

'Many a tale?' Renwick straightened his shoulders. He directed a rather chilly smile over the heads of the group. 'No doubt there might be tales – and ones not so very different from our own. Of course those particular rooms you're looking at have all been re-done. They are expensive places, very well equipped, I should imagine, with all the latest gadgets. You'll find quite young, very well set-up persons living there, I believe. You'll get your dank walls, poor drains, black corners in a good many other places if you care to look. But not up there!'

They had been with him now for half an hour. Renwick had begun to check the various times on their watches with his own, and murmuring: 'I will just make sure,' had walked down the few steps at the far end of the court and out to where, overlooking street and gardens, he could see the large, lit clock at the east end of the city. 'I must be off in five minutes,' he said when he came back, '. . . . letters to attend to . . . a paper to prepare . . .' They asked if he could give them an idea what they should look at the following morning. Briefly he outlined a plan and described the things they should see. They asked if they would meet him again. He explained that he might or might not meet them in a couple of days depending on his work. 'Do you work all through the holidays?' someone innocently asked. Renwick made a non-committal gesture to the sky. At the same time he noticed that the fair-haired girl who'd been wandering about for some time between their group and the shadowy end of the court, had come forward and now stood with them directly under the lamp. Stunning. Not nowadays a word he was in the habit of using. But what other word for this particular kind of fairness? Straight white-blonde hair, fair eyebrows against brown skin, and eyes so pale they had scarcely more colour than water. A Scandinavian – the intonation was clear in a few words she spoke to one of the women, but she was also that idealized version which – along with its opposite – each country holds of another part of the world – strikingly tall, strong and fair – and no doubt outspoken. Renwick waited for her to speak. She lifted her arm with the back of her wrist towards him. She tapped her watch. 'You have given us your minutes. Exactly five. Your time is up,' she said. The others laughed. Renwick smiled. So she had seen his clock-watching, heard his work programme, had simply stopped in passing for a laugh. But attention was now turned her way. They were asking questions. And it appeared that in her country the light was different. The sun, they gathered, was very bright, the darkness more intense. Different, she made it plain, though not of course better. They took it in, unblinking, while they stared. It seemed they got the message on light in a single flash and with no trouble at all. The girl left the place soon afterwards and to Renwick it seemed that his two couples were slowly merged together again, and he with them – all welded into the state called middle-age. No amount of good sense, God-given wisdom or hard-won experience, and least, least of all the beauties of maturity were ever going to mend this matter. There they were. Some light had left them.

One way or another this was to occupy him a good deal during the next day. It was not just that at some stage of life the optimistic beam had been replaced by a smaller light, but that from the start even his awareness of actual physical light had been limited. It was hard for him to imagine variations – how some lights sharpened every object and its shadow for miles around while others made a featureless flatness of the same scene. He tried to imagine those regions of the world made barren to the bone by sun, and others soaked by the same sun to make ground and water prosper from one good year to the next. He thought with relief of white cornfields nearer home and imagined with a shock of hope streams so transparent you could see the fish, leaves and stones shining in their depths.

The phone drilled at his skull. 'Tomorrow evening – would it be possible for half an hour if you can manage to spare the time?' Both couples were leaving the next morning. Yes, it would be just possible to fit it in. They would meet at the bottom of the street leading from Palace to Castle. They would walk slowly up. Another voice joined the first in thanking him.

'The weather has been disappointing for you today,' said Renwick as he waited for the moment to put the phone down.

'No, this is how we like it,' came the reply. 'Clear, sharp, with a touch of frost.' This might pass with those who knew him as a rough description of himself. Or not so rough. Exact perhaps – though some might put the complimentary touch, others a hatching of black lines. Renwick said he was glad to hear it and replaced the receiver thoughtfully.

The next evening was overcast with a slight wind which sent the black and white clouds slowly across the sky. They were waiting for him eagerly. 'A disappointing evening,' he said as if to test them again. On the contrary they were enthusiastic. This was the city at its best, at its most characteristic. Renwick saved his disappointment for himself. They walked slowly up, going in and out of closes, through doors and arches. They saw the sea through openings and climbed halfway up stairways worn into deep curves. Renwick led the way through the darker wynds. He answered questions. Apart from this he said little. The street grew steep, crossed a main road and went on up until it opened out to the broad space in front of the church of St Giles with the Law Courts behind. It was growing dark and from this rise where they were standing they could see down almost the whole length of the street illumined by blue street lights. It was a favourite viewing point for tourist buses and their guides and there were still a few about. People were roaming around the precincts of the Courts and going to and from the church.

Renwick looked round and stared pointedly at the large, lit clock of the Tolbooth, big as a harvest moon. Further down the street were smaller clocks. Automatically following his eyes, the others stared too. They got the message. Time was important even to citizens of an historic city. Things must move on. Turning back again Renwick saw the blonde girl a few steps away. She had been looking at the church. Now she was making a beeline for his group. So he had been watched again, scrutinized no doubt as an exhibit of the place, one worth remembering perhaps, but remembered with a good deal more amusement than respect. She had reached the group now and stood waiting until the couples wandered off to make the most of their last minutes of sight-seeing – then she remarked: 'You have very few angels inside. I have seen the churches. Some of them are very beautiful and very bare.'

'You're absolutely right,' said Renwick. He lectured her gently on the reasons for it. 'Any angels we do have are mostly outside,' he added, 'hidden away in cemeteries.' And if it came to angels it was true enough the blue light had given her own face a marbly shine,

wynd: a very narrow street or passage

her hair a touch of green. But her eyes had neither the exalted nor the downcast look of churchyard angels. They were too direct, too challenging for an angel's eyes. She was not the kind to be hidden away. He was going on to an explanation of the spot where they were standing when something struck him. 'I am not a guide,' said Renwick.

'Well I think you are,' said the young woman. 'You keep them all together. You keep the time. That is important – how you keep the time. Clocks are important, very important indeed. Clocks are – how do you say? – they are very much up your street.' Saying this, she made a quick survey of the street from top to bottom as he had done some minutes before. Her performance managed, miraculously, to be both amiable and derisive. She made way genially for the others when they came back and after some talk with them went off again.

There was nothing to take him out the following evening. Nobody demanded his time. Yet the next night after supper he was out trudging up the High Street again. The place was still crowded and he made his way around groups at corners and through lines of people who were spread out across the width of the street. This time he felt the need to look about him with the eye of a stranger. Many times he stopped to stare at familiar things and once in a while, as if from the corner of his eye, managed to catch some object by surprise. It was a warm night. Far above him he saw rows of elbows upon windowsills and shadowy heads staring down, and above the heads a rocky outline of roofs and steep, black gable walls blocking the night sky. Sometimes he turned back for a closer look at the scrolls or archways or to search for some small stone head over a door. He had become a tourist among tourists, staring at persons and buildings – critical, admiring, sometimes bored, sometimes amazed at what he saw. He grew tired. His own feet looked strange to him as he stepped on and off the kerb or dodged the slippery stones on uneven bits of pavement. He plodded on. His face confronted him, unawares, in dark shop windows, and different from the conscious face in the bedroom mirror. This person looked distraught, looked lonely, battered even, and hardly to be distinguished from some of the down-and-outs who wandered in and out of nearby pubs.

Renwick had come a long way. The Castle was now in view and

it was giving all of them the full treatment. He had seen this often enough – illumined stone and black battlements against a sky still red with sunset. To crown all – a huge, white supermoon breaking through clouds. Renwick found himself in the midst of a large group, all turned that way, all staring as if at a high stage. They were a long time staring. Suddenly, as if at a warning buzz in the brain, Renwick resumed citizenship. He was proud yet impatient of the wide eyes around him. He glanced at his watch, heard his own voice repeat familiar words:

'Yes, that's how it is – very dramatic, very spectacular. Illumined? Yes, very often. The full moon? Yes, don't ask me how – it *seems* often to be full and very well placed, though more romantically speaking than astronomically I would say. You must remember though – we are not only a romantic city. Far from it. Yes, yes, of course there's stuff coming down, but have you seen the new things going up – the business side of things? In other words we are a *busy* people. Time moves on, you see. It moves on here as in every other place.' He looked a man of some consequence, a very busy man with a full timetable to get through. They made way for him. He wished them good-night, passed on.

He was alone now and walking in a quiet side street. The moon and the red sky were behind, the illumination blocked out by high office buildings. He was making for home. Once he stopped in passing for a word with an acquaintance, until they reminded one another of the time and quickly separated. Five persons made up on him and passed, talking animatedly, and Renwick recognized the cadence of this tongue. The blonde girl was walking with three others and a young man. The man was native to the city. The rest, he noted, were all tall, all fair, all dressed with a flair and colour that stood out even in the dark street. If this was the northern myth it was coming over in style. The girl gave him a wave as they went by.

'A fine night,' said Renwick.

'Yes,' the girl called back. 'And how about your moon tonight? Have you looked yet? Has it turned into a clock?' He heard her answering the young man, heard her say in a voice – low, but audible to touchy ears: 'No, no, not moonstruck. He is a time keeper. The man is clock-mad!' She made some remark to the others in her own language. They laughed, looked back over their shoulders and gave him a friendly wave. All five went on their way, noiseless, in rubber soles, and disappeared round the next corner.

But Renwick's shoes were loud on the paving-stones, the footsteps rang in his ears like a metronome. But what were they counting out? Minutes or stones? He stared round once, then turned his back again. This moon had looked cold and white as a snowball. Yet his moonlit ears burned as he walked on.

Getting Used to It

Douglas Dunn

A realistic short story – a slice of life. Or so it seems. It reads almost like a film script, or part of one anyway. But we become more and more involved in the family relationships – unemployed Harry and his wife and their feelings for their growing-up children.

Douglas Dunn is a distinguished Scottish poet but this is from his first (1985) collection of short stories.

Harry Boyle bumped into Vic Nairn on the corner of Hairst Street. 'Harry! Now, you're a sight for sore eyes!' Nairn's cliché greeted Harry with the familiarity of something well known and detested. 'Long time no see!'

'I don't go out much these days, Vic.'

'It's very sad, Harry. But I understand.' Nairn's thin, worn, saddening appearance disguised an iron constitution as ill-health. 'Bob MacQueen was round at my house last week,' he said in his slow, emphatic pronunciation, which was that of a man with a west-of-Scotland accent trying to speak 'properly'. 'We were talking about you. There I was,' he said bitterly, his lips thinning as he drew them against his teeth, 'thinking I was in for a quiet night, with a can of beer, and the TV on, and the wife in the kitchen. When what happens? The doorbell rings. Down to the door, then,' he said wearily. 'And who's there? Bob MacQueen's there. That man depresses me. Oh my God, Harry,' said Nairn in a drawled moan that he seemed to drag up from depths of bilious malice, 'but that's the most miserable man I've ever met!'

'Bob isn't the most generous man I know.' Harry was judicious, for Bob MacQueen was a man he placed in the same category as Vic Nairn. 'And how's your health bearing up, Vic?' Nairn was a man who never said he was well.

'Not too good,' said Nairn. 'Worse.'

'You look well.'

'Do I?' Nairn asked, with the surprise of someone who thinks he knows better. 'Maybe I *look* well . . .'

Harry Boyle was unemployed and, as Nairn knew, he had all the time in the world. He passed some of it taking the family dog for its walks. Having managed to get past Vic Nairn, he risked walking the beast off its little legs by carrying on down King's Road, as if walking off a heavy dinner. Entering High Street on his way home, he caught sight of Bob MacQueen approaching on the same pavement. A change in the traffic lights released a stream of cars, which prevented him from slipping unnoticed across the sreet.

Cursing his luck, he decided he would have to go through with it and hope that MacQueen was in a hurry. MacQueen was a plumber with his own business, and although he had known Harry for years, only a promotion to a white-collar job had made Harry a man to be spoken to in the street and fit for MacQueen's friendship. It was about four-thirty on a day in January, and the rain had stayed off, although everyone in the street was dressed as if expecting to be drenched at any minute. In one of the Co-op's display windows, bedside lamps were aglow on bedside tables. Silent TVs were on in the window next door.

'This is quite a coincidence,' Harry said, forcing himself to be agreeable, tugging his terrier on its leash. It was sniffing around the shopping bag of a displeased woman at the bus stop. 'I've not long been talking to Vic Nairn –'

'I ran into Vic last week,' said MacQueen, as Harry hauled on the leash and the hungry dog skidded across the pavement. 'He was none too steady on his feet. Drink taken, if you ask me. And it doesn't improve him any. But then again, Harry, I ask you this. Who's the man was ever made any better by a guzzle at the hard stuff? Oh my God, Harry, but Victor's the most melancholy man I've ever met! And mean with it.'

'I've certainly seen Vic when he's had things on his mind.'

'Did he say anything about me?'

'He thinks very highly of you.' Harry wondered why he was lying. He wondered too, if MacQueen had really met Nairn, drink taken, in the street, or if, as Nairn claimed, MacQueen had rung Nairn's doorbell.

'The man's a liar if he gives you that impression. I've been in Victor's house, and there he was, sipping a glass of decent whisky' – Harry Boyle smiled, interested – 'and in the course of an hour, an hour,' he repeated, with disbelief and raising his voice, 'not so much as an offer of a drink. Not even a small one from the same bottle as he had by his elbow. It's as if there's but the one glass in the Nairns' house. And I daresay he keeps his teeth in it at night. Mean. *Mean.* A selfish man.' He stared at the pavement, shaking his head in anger at Nairn's inadequate hospitality. 'But he always pours another one, for himself.'

'Drink taken, you say?'

'Drink taken,' MacQueen confirmed. 'As a matter of fact,' he said sadly, 'I've an appointment with the doctor in half an hour. Nasal polyps. Or that's my diagnosis.' He offered a view of his nostrils in the light of the Co-op's display windows. 'And I'm just generally run down. Otherwise I'm OK. But how are chaps like us to know that? If you ask me, we're very much in the hands of the medical profession, Harry. How about you?' he asked without conviction, looking at his watch.

'Health's fine,' said Harry. 'Only problem is, I'm broke, as you can well imagine.'

'Times are hard.' MacQueen looked as if he found other people's problems distasteful. 'It's the same all over.'

When Harry Boyle got home, he found his wife putting her coat on. She had a cleaning job in the High School and worked from five until seven-thirty. Harry kissed her and pulled her collar up while the dog trotted into the living room, dragging its leash.

'That was some walk,' Vera said. 'Is anything wrong?'

'Vic Nairn,' said Harry, 'and then Bob MacQueen. And I had to talk to them. First one,' he said, amused at his own anger, 'and then the other.'

'That'll teach you to walk around the town without looking where you're going.'

They would hear their son, Alan, fussing the dog with dog-chat in the living room.

'Leave Sadie's dinner in the oven,' Vera said. 'And this time, remember to turn it down when you've taken yours out.'

It registered on Harry that in the time he had been on his walk, Vera had cooked the dinner. 'What's Sadie doing this time that she has to be so late?'

'She told you this morning.'

'Did she?'

'She's rehearsing in the school play. She'll be in shortly after six,' she said, kissing him before she went out.

For the past year, the Boyles' son had been behaving with high-spirited secrecy. He was fifteen and looked twenty. The Boyles expected his adolescence to take disturbing contemporary forms, but they were surprised when these came as a jaunty disregard of what they had brought Alan up to believe were the family's conventions. Harry couldn't make up his mind whether to be amused or concerned, silent or censorious. 'You were the same at that age,' Vera had told him. 'So let him get on with it.'

'I was not.'

'I remember you,' she said, 'in winkle-picker shoes and singing a daft song about lollipops on the bus.'

'Me?'

For anyone other than a few friends and a handful of sinister heroes and heroines with mauve hair, neon complexions, and black leather waistcoats with silver studs, Alan exercised a ruthless contempt. 'Walkies? Walkies?' he chirped at the dog, which replied with small barks.

'Y've no intention of taking it a walk,' Harry said.

'Walkies? Walkies?'

'Y' *never* take it a walk!'

'It's my dog.' He fondled the dog roughly by its neck. 'Who's my dog? You're my dog. Aren't you? Walkies?'

'I take it y' know Vic Nairn's son. Alec. That's right, isn't it? Alec? What's Alec Nairn like at school?'

'Walkies?'

'It's got a screw loose. It's been walked stupid. Alec Nairn,' he chivvied. 'I know he's more Sadie's age, but do y' know him?'

'Walkies? Walkies?'

'I've a problem, son,' Harry said. 'Whether to throw you across the room, or that mutt. Alec Nairn! What's he like?'

'Alec Nairn's a zombie.'

'An' Gerald MacQueen? Do y' know *him?* The plumber's boy – do y' know him?'

'Walkies?' Alan sang, the dog's front paws on his lap, its tail wagging frantically.

His father rose from his chair, lifted the dog, crossed the room, opened the door, and placed the terrier in the hall. He closed the door and sat

winkle-picker: very narrow and sharp pointed

down again. Alan stared at him with mock admiration for his decisively paternal action. 'Gerald MacQueen,' Harry reminded him.

'His old man found him down a drain. It's well known. Don't tell me they're running after my sister. I couldn't *stand* it!' He shuddered facetiously and clenched his fists. 'Eat,' he said. 'I've got to eat. I've got to take my mind off it.' He walked away. 'Walkies? Walkies?' Harry heard him say in the hall as the dog barked.

It crossed Harry's mind that the sons of Nairn and MacQueen were probably well-behaved, neat, short-haired, and studious. Alan was short-haired but wore an earring. He gave no impression of being studious, but his marks were a lot higher than his attitude led his parents to expect.

Harry filled his plate and sat at his place at the kitchen table. 'What's on tonight?'

'What day is it?'

'Tuesday.'

'Tuesday night,' said Alan, 'is bondage night.'

Harry was not entirely sure what the word meant, but he had a good idea. 'Whatever bondage is, you eat that up, because this family can't afford to leave food on the plates.'

Alan pushed his half-finished dinner across the table.

'God bless us,' said Harry, exasperated. 'You know more about the world than I do. Don't y'? Watch it, son. You watch your step. That's all I can say.'

Alan walked the kitchen with exaggeratedly careful movements, watching his step.

'I'll give y' a month. An' if y' don't show signs of treatin' your mother an' me to a bit of respect, then you're for the high jump.'

'The high jump? I'm good at the high jump.'

'What I mean, son, is that if I don't see improvements in you along the lines I've mentioned, I'll put your face in.' Alan leaned on the sink, watching his father eat. Harry banged the table with his fist. Alan jumped. 'Just testin' your nerve, son. Face in. Got that?'

Sadie was later than Vera had said. As she ate her dinner, Harry asked, 'Are you sure this play-acting isn't keepin' y' off your studies, girl?' He knew in advance that Sadie would treat his concern as that of a man who left school at fifteen and who had an overstated interest in his daughter's opportunities as a compensation for those he had never had, or had turned down.

'It's Shakespeare. It *is* my studies. *Twelfth Night*,' she said, 'is on the syllabus.'

Harry pointed to the clock on the wall. 'Then what about the hour y' spend sittin' in that café?'

'Do you honestly think that I'm the sort of person who'd waste her time failing exams, when I know how much depends on passing them? Give me credit, Dad. A woman has to show a lot more initiative than a man to get on in this country. The cards are loaded against her.'

'Dice,' said Harry. 'Dice can be loaded, but not cards. Cheats *mark* cards. They don't "load" them.'

'A woman has to be more competent, more qualified than a man, just to get the same job. I know how hard I have to work.'

'Cards aren't loaded. *Dice*.'

'Thanks for the useful information, Dad, but being a topless croupier just doesn't figure in my plans.'

'I don't know what to think. I've a daughter who's into women's rights before she's even left school, and a boy who's into bondage. I'm *mesmerized*.'

'Bondage? Is that what he says?'

'Tuesday night,' said Harry, 'is your brother's bondage night.'

'He doesn't know what it is.'

'Do you know what it is?'

'Of course.'

'Well, sure, of course. You're seventeen, an' this is 1981, so of course y' know. Mind you, I haven't paid much attention to it myself, an' if your mother's given it a thought, then she's kept it quiet, thank God, but you know, an' Alan knows, or Alan says he knows . . . That's fine. *Twelfth Night*'s a Shakespeare? Should I read it before we come and watch you act in it? Assumin', that is, we can afford the tickets. Who do y' play?'

'I play Viola. But most of the time I'm Cesario. And he's a man. If you see what I mean.'

'I think I'd better read it.'

Several days a week, after lunch, Harry and Vera Boyle spent an hour in bed. To begin with, it seemed an extraordinary thing to do, as if, were they discovered, it might bring the unemployed into disrepute.

'I suppose,' Vera said, 'that this is what rich people do in the afternoon. I could get used to it.'

'I'm getting used to it already.' Harry did more housework than he had been brought up to believe was good for a man's dignity. 'How much would it cost,' he asked Vera, 'to have these curtains dry-cleaned?'

'I don't think I like what's happening to you. Last week you washed the kitchen floor, behind my back. And now you're talking about curtains.'

A few days later: 'Have we any carpet shampoo in the house, Vera? I don't see it in the cupboard.'

'Have you spilled something?'

'No. But look at it. It's a good few shades darker than when we bought it.'

Carpet shampoo materialized, as Vera took advantage of Harry's new housewifery, or husbandry.

'I think it's getting to you,' Vera said.

'What is?'

'Unemployment is. And time is, too.'

'You don't hear me talk about unemployment. I just don't get roused by the subject. I've got plenty of time.'

'You were certainly angry enough the night you came home with that redundancy notice.'

'Sure, I was livid. But right now I'm into carpets and curtains. I'm a home boy. If they can keep me on the breadline, plus some, I'll be happy enough and so will you.'

'Guess who's your "plus some".'

'What?'

'Me.' Vera smiled.

As Harry came out of the public park, idling while the dog sniffed the length of the open gate, he saw Vic Nairn leave the swimming baths on the other side of the road. An attendant came half-way down the steps with Nairn, in the posture of a man asking a distressed person if he was sure he would be all right. Curious at the sight of Nairn with a rolled towel under his arm, Harry forgot to hide. Nairn saw him and waved with a limp stroke of his arm, waiting on the pavement for Harry to cross the street.

'I'd no idea you were a baths-goer,' Harry said.

'According to the doctor, I ought to take more exercise. I told him I didn't think it would help my condition. I've seen the day, Harry, when I could manage thirty lengths of the pool and then go for a long run. Remember, when we were boys, how I used to be such a good swimmer?'

Harry could not find these recollections in his mental album of disagreeable episodes involving Nairn as man and boy. 'A powerful swimmer, if I remember correctly, Vic.'

'God, that'll teach me.' Nairn sighed, dolefully resigned to his physical deterioration. 'A length and a half, Harry, and I sank like the Royal Oak. Oh, it was a near thing, Harry. I've been at death's door before now, as you well know, but that's the first time I've seen the doorman. And I know what you're thinking. Why's a hardworking man like me to be seen coming out the baths on a Friday afternoon? I'm on short time. Me, on short time!'

'I'm very sorry to hear that, Vic.' Harry worried at his own sincerity.

'Twenty-four years I've given that company. They'll be closing,' said Nairn, sonorous with industrial gloom. 'I give them three months at the very most. I don't know what I'll do. And there's the humiliation coming, the affront of it all, of having to sign on for the dole, for the unemployment benefit!'

'You'll get used to it,' Harry said encouragingly.

'Do you have to stand in a queue, with other men? What I mean is,' he whispered, 'is it possible – I mean, is there a time when they're not busy? You'll know this, Harry. Can I pop in,' he asked furtively, holding Harry by the elbow, 'without having to stand in a queue?'

'They'll give you a time, Vic,' Harry said.

'We'll not see the likes of Bob MacQueen in a dole queue,' said Nairn, his lips smacking with vindictiveness.

'If he goes bust,' said Harry, 'it's the end of the world. MacQueen's self-employed. He isn't entitled to unemployment benefit.'

'He'll have made provisions,' said Nairn. 'But even so, here's hoping,' he said, his eyes widening, 'that the bottom falls out of the plumbing trade.'

'I wouldn't go that far,' said Harry, jerking the dog on its leash, angry with himself for having given so much as a hint of complicity in Nairn's bad-mindedness. 'No, y' wouldn't say a thing like that if you'd been unemployed for as long as I have.'

'Oh, don't say that, Harry. I'll find a job. I'll *look* for one.'

'I looked as well, y' know.'

'I didn't mean it like that, Harry.'

'It's new to you, Vic. But you'll find out.' He was pleased at having bad tidings of his own to pass on, but checked himself from rubbing them in.

'It's the indignity of it!'

'Forget that,' said Harry. 'Believe me, it'll pass. Think of all the time you'll have to spend with Mrs Nairn.'

'Oh God, no.'

'Must make tracks, Vic. Big night out, Sadie's got the star part in *Twelfth Night.*'

'My boy Alec's more or less masterminding that!' Nairn's anxious mood changed to one of enthusiastic pride.

'He is?' Pained by this news, Harry persevered in making his escape. 'Must go. See y' soon, Vic.'

'I'll see you tonight!' Nairn shouted after him, the near-drowning, short time, and threat of no time banished.

In his suit, his white shirt, his best tie, and his best shoes dotingly polished, Harry joined Alan in the living-room. He studied his languorous son. 'Shakespeare was never up my street, either. But y' could've made the effort. It's your sister I'm going to see, no' Shakespeare. In fact, she plays a man, Cesario, as well as Viola. Same person, really – Viola pretends, y' see, an' dresses up as a man. I would've thought *that* was right up your street. An' look at the trouble your mother's gone to. She's taken her togs in a bag, and she's changing at the school, after three hours' hard work on her knees scrubbin' floors.' Harry started temperately and ended up losing his patience. 'What's on tonight, then? An' before y' ask, it's Friday.'

'I'm in love,' Alan said cynically. 'I'm staying in to wash my hair, and pine.'

During the first interval, after Act II, Harry and Vera stood together drinking coffee from plastic cups in the corridor outside the school's theatre. They smiled at nearby couples. 'Did you scrub this?' Harry asked her.

'We don't scrub it. It's parquet,' she said. 'We do it with a mechanical polisher.'

'Who taught Sadie to speak like that? She sounded . . . well, she sounded English.'

'That's what I've been wondering.'

'What did you think?'

'I think she's terrific.'

'But dressed up as a man, wearing a man's clothes – it gave me the fright of my life, love.'

'Don't drip coffee,' Vera chided, 'on my parquet.'

'We'll have to keep an eye out,' said Bob MacQueen, joining them, accompanied by his wife. 'I caught a view there of Victor Nairn.'

'What did you think of Gerald, Mrs Boyle?' asked Mrs MacQueen, overdressed, large, and proud. 'Malvolio,' she said. 'Of course, we won't get the best of Malvolio until a little later. Awfully funny, isn't he?'

'Oh, Malvolio! Harry, Gerald's playing Malvolio,' Vera said, with a nudge, as if this were good news.

'What's worrying me,' said MacQueen, anxiously looking round in case Vic Nairn had spotted them in the crowd, 'is that this fairy-tale stuff could go to Gerald's head. Not to mention how much this is costing the ratepayers. Harry these costumes alone . . . Oh God, the sight of my own son dressed up like an idiot,' MacQueen said, in agony, 'gives me a *pain*.'

'It's a comedy,' said Vera.

'I'm not laughing,' said MacQueen. 'Even if this is Shakespeare, it's just a frill, an extra, and in days like these – well, I don't have to tell you, Harry.'

'Business not too good, Bob?' Harry asked, while their wives attempted to submerge their pride in seriousness.

'Business, Harry, is downright awful. I could do with a real cold snap. I need burst pipes. Another mild winter and I don't know what I'll do. And who can afford to install central heating these days? And these nasal polyps? The doctor had the cheek to say I must have broken my nose at some time. Now, if a man had broken his nose, he'd know about it. Wouldn't he? I ask you, Harry . . .' They went into the theatre as the second bell rang and schoolgirls ushered the audience to its seats. 'There's something up these nostrils of mine, Harry. I just know it.' Harry closed his eyes. He had more than a fair notion of what, or who, was getting up his own nose. 'Any pains yourself, Harry?'

'Not a pain exactly,' Harry said. 'More a sort of a dull ache, at the back of my neck.'

Once seated, Vera said, 'Not a word about Sadie. It was Gerald, Gerald, Gerald. And our Sadie has the best part. She's marvellous. But not so much as a mention.'

'Oh, no,' said Harry, 'he's seen us.' He returned a wave to Vic Nairn, convinced he would be denied the chance of avoiding him later. 'Who's his boy playing? Belch? Aguecheek?'

' "Assistant Stage Manager",' Vera read from the programme, as the lights were dimmed too quickly and then came up again.

In this fresh burst of light, Harry took the programme. 'That figures. He's in charge of the lighting.' He waved again at the Nairns, this time in a better frame of mind.

Backstage noises were audible, until an urgent voice hushed them. The lights dimmed and then came up again. The curtain rose a few feet – enough to show Viola's legs and the spangled tights of Feste the Clown. Then it dropped like a gesture of irritation. The audience mumbled with polite concern. Older schoolboys stamped their feet. Several hearties let off piercing whistles.

'It's such a pity,' said the woman sitting on Harry's left. 'They've been doing *awfully* well up to now.'

Vera leaned over and said good evening to the couple.

'Our son,' said the husband, 'is Orsino, the Duke of Illyria.'

'Our daughter,' said Vera, 'is Viola. And Cesario.'

'How lovely! They'll be getting married, you know,' said the woman they had never seen before.

'Not at this rate they won't be,' said Harry.

'What's happening? Have you any idea why it's being delayed like this?' asked the woman.

'I've a strong suspicion,' said Harry, 'that the assistant stage manager is a bit like his father.'

Lights dimmed, the curtain rose. 'Save thee, friend, and thy music,' Viola greeted the Clown. 'Dost thou live by thy tabor?'

'No, sir,' said Feste, sitting on his drum, 'I live by the church.'

'Our daughter,' Harry said to Vera, 'is an absolute knockout. She's got a future in this racket.'

Having Taken Off My Wheels

Martin Elliott

Massed-start cycle races have been seen on TV – but not often! So the 'hero' of this story is (was?) devoted to very much a minority sport. Perhaps he has now changed his devotion!

Martin Elliott has been having stories published since the 1970s. His recent interests have been academic, with a doctor's degree for a study of Shakespeare's *Othello*. He does not say where he got his knowledge of the world of this story.

I must (deride me not) be somewhere where I can, without disaster, bicycle.
Henry James, 4 February 1896

For your internal ears and eyes I give you Celia itemized – in her surfaces as she would wish to be, complete, with her two hands and her ten toes. She is slender, small-stepping. She strolls, you might say, from the hips while her head, motionless, schoons along on the pole of her neck. Unknown to Celia, her feet have the slightest of tendencies to indicate out; and this makes her endearing. She is brunette and wears her hair either down to her eyebrows or brushed back. But the hygiene of her head is more problematical: every fifth day her hair is washed with cream; on the other days, however, she brushes it with a dry shampoo – by this same principle do hens take dust-baths. As a result her hair is fine but faded, a dry umbrella-black. Her skirts and dresses she mostly buys in brooch-like shops in suburbs and small towns. As for her physical measurements, Celia would not mind my telling that she is five foot four on her naked soles. Her sectional dimensions, though, I shall not divulge. Suffice it, that her pectoral inches are exactly those of her pelvic ones and that her waist is a centimetre less than my right thigh at rest. Is it any wonder, then, that Celia as she walks is a causer of minor collisions at traffic lights?

It was during one of these accidents that Celia first encountered me. First, I have to say that I am a part-time first-category professional massed-start racing cyclist. You will find me, if ever you take the trouble, of a Sunday after lunch in season, amazing the townspeople of Stevenage, Welwyn and such with my forty-mile-an-hour finishes up their roped-off High Streets at the back of a police car's siren. My confrères and I bring a dash of colour – our several team jerseys being a medley of unamalgamated reds and yellows, park-greens and budgerigar-blues – to the inhabitants of various English Sundays. However, we competitors are unillusioned about the lip-service of the walls of leaning bodies and megaphone hands that we sprint between. We would lack their support were it a soccer time of year. This is why so many of us *coureurs cyclistes*, participants in one of this country's minority sports, are so cynical, not to say paranoiac. And this is why I reacted in such a boomerang manner on that Saturday in March when Celia, idling over Great Russell Street as if she were Nefertiti among her double-parked slaves, caused me to swerve and crash, still in my scarab position, head down and arms semi-extended, into the spear-like railings of the British Museum (which exhibits, I learned later, not even a penny farthing) with the sort of impact I'd have had if I'd pedalled down the side of a pyramid and hit the Sphinx.

I confronted her.

'Are you vending something?' she frowned at the W H KRISPS sign that I wear across the chest of my jersey in return for being sponsored by that as yet little known manufacturer of foodstuffs.

She informed me when she knew me better, 'In your what d'you call them? black training tights you looked like a cross between Rudolf Nureyev and Max Wall. Most unusual.'

What charmed me was her contrition. She watched me take my wheels off and push my frame into the rear of her hatchback that was round the corner on a yellow line. Before driving me back to Hertfordshire she took me to her flat where I had a shower and placed Savlon on all the protuberances of my body's left side – cheekbone and shoulder, elbow and hip, knee and ankle; all these having hit the pavement one by one in ascending order. As I did this I heard her playing an upright piano in the living-room which

Max Wall: a comedian very much in the music-hall tradition. Noted for the remarkable way he can contort body and features
Savlon: the trade name of an antiseptic ointment

was lined, as if for warmth, with books. Most of these books were weighty ones, and a lot of them were about ancient civilizations. There were even two shelves of books about Egypt in the lavatory. There was an unusual quietness about the lavatorial gulp; and as I came out the cistern discreetly chuckled. Celia gave me tea and then drove me home. The next day she telephoned to inquire how I was enduring my bruises, and inside the week I was deploying her legs into the semblance of a speedway cycle's upright handlebars and then into the shape of drops.

The Tree House

Ronald Frame

Ronald Frame is another Scot but lives in London. He is a novelist and short story writer and has recently been making a further name for himself as author of plays for broadcasting.

Are children 'adults without any softening graces'? Can children be evil? What makes Alan the way he is? What will he be like when he is an adult?

They were walking down Drayton Gardens, the two of them. I saw them from the other side of the road and stood behind a tree tying my shoelace till they'd passed. I was perched on one leg, shaking. They disappeared into a block of mansion flats.

I crossed the road and watched the windows from behind another tree. The lights went on in a room in one of the middle floors. She walked over to the balcony doors and looked out. He was pouring drinks at the sideboard: I could just see the tops of an armada of bottles. He handed her a glass and she took it without looking at him. Maybe he put music on because she started moving her hips. She was still watching the length of the street. Could she have seen me? But if she was hoping for another look to confirm it really had been me, she gave up soon enough. She pivoted on her high heels, swinging round in her silks to give herself to whatever domestic life they lived now like tamed savages in the quiet heart of Chelsea.

We were children together once. There was Alan – and Claire – and me. I think Alan – and Claire, by complicity – were the evilest people I've ever known. Were, are. (I didn't even think of ourselves then, when it happened, as *children*; I didn't make that prime mistake of presuming we were innocent. A child is an adult without any

Chelsea: a district in London, mostly fashionable, known for the shops in the King's Road and for its annual Flower Show

softening social graces – but given an intensity of character which the years seem to take away from you. That intensity can be terrifying. At the time those two filled my perspective as fully as any grown-up did.)

Our families lived in a small Wiltshire town with an abbey, famous for its picture-postcard looks. Alan's father was a senior partner in a law firm, and did court work in Winchester; he was well known for the sharpness of his brain and won all his cases (even, it was said, when he had the proof his client was guilty). His wife was his only failure to date. She'd done an unheard-of thing: she'd run away. I heard my mother and her friends discussing her, exchanging the rumours – someone thought they'd seen her (or her double) attending in Harrods' haberdashery; and because they knew her mother lived in Hove, another time they decided she'd fled to Brighton for a gadfly life and she'd already been disgraced in some unmentionable way. Claire's father was the second-in-charge at the abbey, and decency personified; her roly-poly French mother feelingly played Debussy on the piano at amateur concerts fund-raising for the roof. My father was a doctor; my mother was a scion of ancient, inbred blue-blood stock, she raised me (rather tiredly) and belonged (indifferently) to the West of England League of Lily-Growers and had afternoon bridge sessions in the house when she could summon the energy to spin the dial on the phone to muster her friends. This only matters set against the truth of our three characters, what our lives had made us: Alan – pushy and masterful like his father in the courtroom, impatient, unscrupulous, unforgiving; Claire – sensitive and thoughtful and conciliating like her decent father, but in the end fickle and weak; and me – I don't know what, nothing very much, careful, hesitant, testing, uncommitted, and at the mercy of them both.

We were supposed to become friends simply because we lived in genteel houses on the same pretty street. But the houses dated back

Harrods: a famous London department store
Brighton: a seaside resort, sometimes called 'London by the Sea'. Hove is also by the sea and is completely joined to Brighton
blue-blood: said to be a feature of the aristocracy. The term comes from Spain and originally described, in the days of the Moorish kingdoms in Spain, Europeans through whose pale skin the blue veins could be seen

centuries and were built like little palazzi, fortresses with high honeystone walls and railings and gates and hedges, and for all we normally saw of other people's existences we could have been living fields apart from them. There was also such a thing as a residents' association recently got together to keep Foss Street pretty and in the 'right hands' and to judge on the colours of front doors, and really our intended 'friendship' so-called was just a consequence of that inspired gesture of adult self-interest.

My mother invited Alan to our house one day, a few months after his own mother's flight. She prodded me in the shoulder when she introduced us so I'd take him outside into the garden. (It meant I was to be 'nice' to him.) Claire, who was my friend already, looked as embarrassed as I was feeling myself. The three of us played Grandma's Footsteps – 'What's the time, Mr Wolf?' – but Alan was rather rough about it and had great delight catching us both. Claire and I had to sit down by the little pond for a breather.

It was Alan, standing over us watching us, who suggested it – out of the blue. 'We'll build a tree house!' Claire said she'd never heard of a 'tree house'. I'd seen a photograph of the bush hotel on stilts where the Queen stayed in Kenya on her honeymoon and I thought of that. He decided the first fork on the old oak would be ideal. He ran back with us to ask my parents. They said 'yes, of course', with kindly smiles for Alan's motherless condition.

It took a few days to build. It also gave Alan unlicensed access to my garden. At the weekend my father found us lengths of wood he hammered together to make a platform, with four more planks for a balustrade on each side. (Banging away, he told us there was a tradition of having bedrooms upstairs in houses because our ancestors, the cavemen, used to make *their* sleeping places in trees to be safe from predators. 'Animals?' I asked him. 'Yes. Or humans,' he said.) Claire contributed some lopped branches from a pine tree in the vicarage garden: they still had their needles attached, and Alan without discussing it arranged them to make a chalet-style roof to give us shade. My father knotted some chandler's cable-rope to one of the other branches. Then it was more or less complete and ready. Claire's mother gave us two tins of condensed milk and a packet of

Grandma's Footsteps: a children's game. One child stands face towards a wall. The others try to creep up and touch him or her without being seen. The same game is also called *Peep behind the Curtain* or *Sly Fox*

Playbox biscuits to fortify us. We thought the biscuits were a bit juvenile: we were seven and would have appreciated digestives, or ginger nuts, which are harder and you can nibble at longer.

We had the 'opening' one afternoon when my parents were out and the help didn't see me removing the soda syphon from the sideboard. Claire squirted it at the trunk and said the proper words, gleaned from abbey fête-openings. I followed Alan's lead – but less earnestly – clapping and whistling. Then we each shinned up the trunk. My shoulders strained with the unaccustomed exercise. When we were up the three of us sat down, but awkwardly. There was something not quite right. It wasn't just the seasick feeling: maybe it was because the planning and anticipation were over and we realized this was what it had been in aid of and we didn't know how to begin. Claire smiled sweetly at us, how her mother smiled on her charity musical evenings. I smiled too – in the vague way my mother did when she welcomed her professional bridge friends to the house. Alan didn't smile. (Was it because he'd forgotten how *his* mother used to smile, I wondered – if she ever had?) He just watched us; he wouldn't stop looking at us, his eyes flicked between us. Claire had phoned me up about the pine branches in her garden without letting him know, and I thought he must have taken it as a slight. Much more than that, I can see now – it had been read as a deliberate cut, a prearranged snub, an insult, a scornful challenge to his kingship. That was Alan. He could always imagine things were any number of times worse than they really were. Sitting there cross-legged his anger seemed to be consuming him. I was fixed by the pull of his eyes. From her to me, me to her, her to me, me to her. (Was it a habit he'd picked up from his unhappy parents, when he sat witness to the public-room silences like adjournments between their prosecution bouts upstairs we used to hear with our windows open, which my mother called their 'blow-outs'? You couldn't be sorry for him, though: Alan wasn't like that. I knew that even my expertly diplomatic parents could only spare him their tender smiles, not their sympathy. Already at seven he was ringed with barbed wire; his eyes hooked into you, tore flesh.) I think that for something so very little – Claire telling me first about the axed branches instead of him – he hated me.

I don't use the word lightly. My mother always forbade me to say it. 'You dislike something strongly . . .' she told me. I'm not sure what the difference was: maybe it sounded more elegant and less raw, put that way. But Alan didn't just 'dislike strongly'. Hating is a trait of paranoia, it fixes on the object, it belongs to an obsessive nature. His mother's days – until she abandoned husband and son – had been spent keeping the house as antiseptically dustless as a space capsule: in the evenings she would have to lie down in the bedroom with a migraine and that's when the famous quarrels began. That's how it began with Alan too, the inherited oddness, and then his father telling him (when she could hear) that his mother was off-the-beam.

The anger happened again about something else. I was used to the talk of my mother and her friends about that mania for cleanliness and order driving Alan's father to a frenzy – so now their home without anyone to look after them was reputed to be a midden of unmade beds and unwashed dishes. After several visits to the tree house, Claire started in like vein. She announced in a lecturing voice that we ought to have a 'system' about things: for instance we should scrape the mud off our sandals before we climbed off the rope. She insisted the biscuits should be kept *there* and the top must always be kept tightly shut on the tin. Alan was hating it, his eyes flared at her. I took her side, by instinct I suppose, and said we needed 'discipline'. He told me very quietly – but spitting the words at me – to 'sod off'. He must have heard his father use the expression to his mother. It was new to Claire and me, although it sounded angry and we could guess its rudeness from the tone. I was feeling that incidents like this could only make the two of us closer, Claire and me (even when we weren't *meaning* to hurt him). Alan was smart enough to spot the complicity starting for himself. Claire – patching up – asked him to open one of our two precious tins of condensed milk with the tin opener. He saw through that ruse. 'Ask *him*,' he told her, his eyes tightening on me. 'You can have one of your own,' she said to placate him, with a new energy and desperation in her voice. But he wasn't listening to her and got up and swung off down the rope. (He was easily the best at that. He'd seen a Tarzan film on television. Neither of us – see how I make the association? – neither Claire nor I in our separate homes were allowed to watch television as indiscriminately as he did.)

'Anyway,' I shouted after him, stuck for anything else to say, 'it's *my* garden.' It sounded crass and stupid and the words seemed to float in the air without going away. He walked over and started to jump up and down on the rope, drumming his fists on the boards of our floor. The house rocked, like a boat on waves. Claire screamed and clutched my arm. 'Please, please tell him to stop!' I didn't want to tell him any such thing. He kept thumping his fists on the planks. 'Oh, make him stop!' I didn't know what to do. I couldn't let him get away with the outrage, but I realized things were just about over between us and I wanted it to be all *his* doing, not mine. I was determined. (Can you be determined at seven? Why not, as at twenty-seven or seventy-seven?) The raft of planks we were standing on began to tilt. The blows shuddered up through my legs. Claire was in tears, waving at him. 'Please stop, please stop! *Alan*!'

And it stopped. That was all he was wanting her to do – say his name. I shut my eyes, opened them again: I'd thought I was going to be sick with the motion. In a moment he was perfectly gentle and he was helping her to slide down the rope. She was shaking and had to lean on him. I blinked at the two of them walking off together through the haze of summer insects.

Another afternoon there was a domestic mix-up: I was supposed to be going to Salisbury with my parents after lunch, but something happened and we stayed at home. I climbed up into the tree house, which my father had made safe again, and called at the top of my voice over the orchard into Claire's parents' walled garden. She was outside and heard me and did a Red Indian whoop. 'Tell Alan!' I cried to her. Claire whooped and shouted 'Alan!' in the other direction, but her voice wouldn't have been strong enough to carry that extra distance. I think I knew that when I asked her. I'd never tried these jungle calls before (the information came from Alan, watching Johnny Weissmuller on television). But I understood straight away what the significance of this novel method of communication was, that the weakness of Claire's voice gave me an excellent means of excluding Alan any time I didn't want him.

So Claire came on her own and we had a pleasant afternoon up in the tree, out of sight of the house. We chatted and compared our

Salisbury: a cathedral city in Wiltshire, south-west of London
Johnny Weissmuller: an American athlete who played the part of Tarzan in early film versions

shadows slowly lengthening on the grass towards the pond. We lay on our backs and listened to the lazy hum of insects under us. We must have started to doze because we were invaded before we seemed to understand what was happening. One moment tranquillity and contentment with our day, the next Alan flying off the end of the rope and the tree house was an echo-box. 'A-*ha*!' He stamped a war dance with his bare feet, laughing at the shock on our faces. He was dressed up like a crazy pirate. He had red stuff like lipstick smeared on his cheeks and a curtain ring over one ear and a bright yellow towel for a cummerbund. 'Well, well, well!' It sounded just like his father talking to his mother, when his voice used to travel to us on a still night and before she packed her bags and ran away. He pushed on my chest with his foot so I couldn't get up. 'Well, well, *well*!' He kept saying it, smiling down into my face. But none of this was meant to be fun.

He bent over me and dragged me across the platform by my arms. I tried scraping my heels on the floor like brakes then twisting my bottom from side to side to slow him, but nothing could have succeeded against his strength and purpose. My head was suddenly hanging over the edge with empty space underneath. 'Well, well, *well*!' He wasn't laughing any more. Claire called to him to stop. He told her 'Shut your mouth!' Then I seemed to be back inside again, on all-fours, and he was booting me in the bottom chanting, 'Out! Out! Out!' Claire had her hands on his shoulders. 'Please don't, Alan! Please don't!' He flung the rope at me: I held on but I was shaking like jelly and when I slithered down it went burning through my palms. I fell on my back on the grass and the pain made me start to cry. Alan had landed behind me and was yelling at Claire to come down. He grabbed my arm and began to pull me like a dead body. I saw where he was making for, the pond. 'Go on, take his legs!' Claire came running after us. 'What are you going to do?' 'Take his legs! Do as I say or I'll throw you in too!' I don't suppose she felt she had any choice and she tried to lift my weight; she couldn't and dropped my legs and then picked them up again when Alan said he would twist her arm. He called her a 'bloody woman' and she burst into tears at such foulness. She let me go and Alan pulled me the rest of the way, quicker so he didn't lose his resolve. I believe that at seven he had the badness in him to know I would be his revenge on the world.

As I tried scrambling up off the flagstones, hands pushed into my aching back which sent me pitching forwards again. I could hear screams and shouts from my mother and her bridge friends who'd seen. I crashed into the water and the cold was like splitting ice. My eyes opened and I seemed to be tumbling through space, passing stars. My arms must have floated up and the rest of me too, for after the blackness I was on my back seeing a blue summer sky shining absurdly far away from me. The branches of the tree were like cracks in a blue plate. Then between me and them I saw two faces peering down, the crazy pirate's, and the one behind with a wondering look. Out of the sky two arms came reaching into the water, but not (as I thought it must be) to save me. They seemed to want to hold me down, not help me up. The striped face dropped closer, and at one point I was making the connection, that the arms belonged to *him*. Alan. His white hands fluttered above me like sea anemones in a swell. I felt them fastening on my neck and I tried in the coldness to find them with my own hands. I locked them on something but I didn't know any more if it was him or me. I'd gone down and bobbed up again and my head must have made a hole in the water because I could hear the panic of high voices. I think I went down again – or twice more – before there was an explosion of water and through it other arms were reaching in to rescue me. I felt a different kind of strength in them, and I gave myself willingly.

They laid me on the grass and it was what I saw when I could open my eyes to observe the world – the tree house – above their heads, beyond their concern, where the clouds seemed to have torn to fleece on the oak's branches. It was riding the afternoon very precariously. A sudden wind might bring it down. My mother saw me looking. 'Daddy'll repair it,' she said through tears and she tried to make me more comfortable till he came, brushing off insects with her scented handkerchief.

If he does repair it, I was thinking, I live in it alone this time. I saw afternoons ahead, and books, and biscuits, and watching into people's rooms and never being seen. For a moment, with the sun finding me through the grid of branches and warming my face, I seemed to be picking wisdom ripe out of that blue air.

Up-Ladle at Three

William Glynne-Jones

This story, perhaps surprisingly, for it is set in a Welsh steel works, was first published in the *New Yorker*. In a different way from the previous story, this, too, is a suspense item. Was it an accident? Or was it murder? And if so, why?

The story is very much based on experience of the working people of the Welsh valleys in the days, not so long ago, when steel works and coal mines were a way of life.

The men in the steel works are working close to the foundry, where the steel is molten. They prepare moulds into which they pour the white-hot liquid steel to make 'castings'. It is tough work and can be dangerous if anyone makes a mistake.

Squint, the foreman moulder, stood with arms folded on the wooden planks covering the heavy-castings' pit. He peered at the men as they bustled around in the casting bay, getting the moulds ready.

'Get a move on,' he rasped. 'It's up-ladle at three. You've got ten minutes left. Hey, you – Owen and Ritchie! Close that spindle.' He pointed to a mould, its top and bottom half contained in two steel boxes, approximately seven feet long by three wide and three deep. 'Make sure the joints match,' he muttered. 'We don't want any more complaints from the main office.'

The young moulder named Owen eyed the foreman quizzically. 'You don't intend casting that spindle, do you?'

Squint frowned. 'What d'you mean? What's wrong with it?'

'Have a *decko* at this.' Owen drew a finger over a deep crack in the box. 'This moulding-box isn't safe.'

'You can't tell me what to damn well do!' Squint shouted. 'That spindle's got to be cast today, so get it closed . . . Ritchie Bevan!'

have a decko: have a look. *Dekko* is a Hindi word brought back by British soldiers from India. There are many English words from that source

Ritchie, sandy-haired, with a candid face, looked at the foreman. 'Yes?'

'Close that mould. The furnace's waiting.'

'I tell you this box isn't safe,' Owen insisted. 'Ritchie and I won't be responsible if anything happens. So to hell with you!'

The foreman looked wildly around.

'Evan! Bill!'

Evan-Small-Coal and Bill Taylor hurried across.

'Yes, Mr Brewer?'

'Get that spindle ready. I want it for the afternoon's cast.'

The two moulders jumped promptly to obey his orders, and Squint spun round to face Owen once more. 'You'll answer for this, both of you.' He raised his hand threateningly.

Ritchie sprang forward and gripped him by the sleeve. 'Shove that fist back in your pocket, Brewer. It's lucky for you we're in the foundry, else I'd ha' stretched you out flatter'n a pancake.'

Squint opened his mouth to say something when suddenly a stentorian cry from the furnace landing echoed through the foundry.

'Up-ladle, Da-a-a-i!'

Owen pulled Ritchie aside. 'Aw, come on. Let's get out of this,' he snapped, 'I'm fed up to the teeth.'

They crossed the heavy-castings' pit and stood near a water *bosh*. Squint shook his fists at them. 'I'll see you'll suffer for this,' he shouted. 'You know damn well there's not the slightest risk.'

He swung around to the two moulders who were closing the spindle mould. 'Put a jerk into it, you fellers,' he bellowed.

The top half of the mould had been lowered, the joints sealed, and the flanges secured by a row of steel cramps wedged with triangular pieces of scrap iron. The spindle was then raised to an upright position and placed on a bed of dry sand. Two piles of boxes placed on each side of it supported a wooden plank for the *teemer* to stand upon.

Meanwhile, the furnace had been tapped. The ladle, with its fifty tons of molten steel, swung above the spindle mould. The crane-man, Dai Jones, shielded his eyes from the fierce glare as he peered over the edge of his steel cage and waited for his instructions.

The *teemer* scrambled up the pile of boxes facing the spindle. He

bosh: an old term in iron making. It is a trough for cooling the hot steel
teemer: the man who empties the molten steel into the moulds

sank to his knees on the wooden staging and reached for the nozzle lever.

'Swing her over an inch to furnace, Dai!' Squint called.

The crane's control levers clicked.

'Okay. Let her go!'

The *teemer* pulled downwards: the white-hot steel rushed in a circular stream from beneath the ladle and dropped into the spindle with a hollow thud. A red tongue of flame shot into the air, and the gurgling, boiling metal rose slowly to the brim of the mould.

Bill Taylor climbed up over the boxes. As the ladle swayed along to the next mould, he tilted a bucketful of powdered blacking on to the bubbling steel and prodded the thick crust with a long iron rod.

He looked across to the water *bosh*.

'Hey, Ritchie! You keeping an eye on this spindle?'

Ritchie stepped up to him. 'It's your job, not mine. You closed it.'

'I didn't want the job, did I?' Bill grumbled.

'If Squint asked you to take a running jump into the ladle, you'd do it,' Ritchie said. 'If anything happens . . .' He held out his hands expressively. 'It's not my pigeon.'

The cast was over, and the empty ladle was swung back to its bed beneath the furnace landing. Shoulders drooped, head bowed, the perspiring *teemer* walked to the water *bosh* where Owen stood. He glanced sideways at the young moulder. 'What's eating Brewer?' he asked. 'Had a bit of a rumpus with him, didn't you?'

Owen did not reply.

'Okay, if that's how you feel.' The *teemer* shuffled back towards the empty ladle. All at once he wheeled sharply around, his eyes wild with fear. He rushed to the *bosh* and grasped Owen's shoulder.

'Look, man . . . the spindle. It's – it's running out! Ritchie's down there . . . trapped, like a bloody rabbit.'

A wild, piercing scream cleaved the air. Bill Taylor leaped headlong from the wooden staging. 'Help! For God's sake . . . Help!' he shouted, frantically. 'Give us a hand, quickly . . . The spindle's burst!'

Owen pushed the agitated *teemer* violently aside and raced over the pit. He stumbled into the casting bay. Suddenly he stopped.

Before him, his eyes dilated with terror, stood Ritchie on one foot, precariously balanced on a single brick near the centre of a rapidly filling pool of white-hot metal. Momentarily the foot slipped from the brick, and he screamed.

'Mam! Oh, Jesus Christ, Christ! Mam! Mam!' Ritchie's agonizing cries shrieked above the thunder of the cranes as they grated to a standstill on the quivering girders. A pungent smell of roasted flesh hung in the fetid air. The yellow flames bit into his hands and face. Paralysed with fear and pain he shrieked continuously, loudly and terrifyingly.

'Do something, one of you!' Owen yelled to the horror-stricken moulders in the bay. He caught Bill Taylor by the arm. 'Phone the doctor! Hurry, for God's sake!'

Without further hesitation he threw a board over the space, tore off his jacket and darted forward. Throwing it around the tortured Ritchie's body, he grasped him in his arms and dragged him to safety.

Gently he laid him on the ground. The crowd of men, whispering and gesticulating, closed in around the prostrate figure.

'Give him air!' Owen cried. He threw out his arms and braced his shoulders against the crowd. He glanced apprehensively around. 'Where's Bill? Has the doctor come?'

'Make way there,' someone called authoritatively. The crowd parted. The foundry's first-aid man, followed by two others carrying a stretcher, pushed his way to the front. From a small box he took out a bottle of greenish liquid, pads of cotton wool and rolls of bandage. He called the stretcher-bearers to his side.

'Easy, now.'

One of the men placed his hands under Ritchie's legs. A charred boot crumbled at his touch, pieces of brown, roasted flesh adhering to it. The man retched. His face turned a sickly green. His hands slipped down Ritchie's trousers and came in contact with the raw, shining heel bone.

Ritchie whimpered with pain. His fingers clawed wildly at Owen's shoulders. The skin of his closed eyelids was blistered, the eyelashes singed. His face, a dirty yellow, drawn and haggard, glistened with cold sweat. Now and again he shivered convulsively.

Owen tenderly raised his injured friend to a sitting position.

'Ritchie . . . Ritchie,' he choked. He looked into the first-aid man's face. 'It's too late, too late,' he sobbed. 'Nothing can be done.'

Ritchie stared at him vacantly. His fingers and lips moved. He coughed weakly.

'A fag,' he whispered. 'A . . . fag.'

A cigarette was placed between his lips; it fell from his mouth and rolled to the ground.

Owen pillowed Ritchie's head on his knees and stared wild-eyed at the gaping crowd.

'He's dead! Dead – d'you hear me?' he shouted. 'Ritchie's dead . . . murdered by a butcher of a foreman . . . D'you hear me, fellers? My pal Ritchie's been murdered!'

One of the men stooped down and patted Owen's hand.

'Calm down, Owen. You don't realize what you're saying,' he whispered nervously. 'It was an accident, as you can see. All the men here can testify that it couldn't be helped, and . . .'

Owen rose slowly to his feet. His teeth were clenched. His eyes burned. He grasped the speaker by the shoulder and shook him fiercely.

'Accident!' he shouted. 'Accident!'

The man spluttered. 'Such things happen, don't they?' He pulled away, his eyes full of fear.

Presently Squint shouldered his way into the ring. 'Get that box out into the scrap yard,' he ordered. 'Smash the damn thing!'

'Oh, no you don't.' Owen wheeled round to face the foreman. 'There's a hell of a lot of questions to be asked before this affair is cleared. And that box will answer all of them.'

Squint pretended not to have heard.

'How – how's Ritchie?' he asked.

'He's dead!' The words were cold and harsh.

The foreman paled. 'Dead? But I – I thought he was saved?'

'Saved?' Owen mocked. 'Saved?' He stepped up to the foreman, his fists clenching and unclenching. 'You damned murderer!' he raged. 'You killed him!'

Squint edged back. 'Keep him away,' he appealed to the men. 'He's out of his mind.'

Owen leapt forward and clutched him by the throat. 'I'll strangle you . . . you swine,' he hissed between his bared teeth. He glared at the men. 'You saw what happened? You heard me warn him, didn't you?'

No one answered.

'God! Isn't there a man amongst you? Are you going to stand by and see your mate murdered, without a word in protest?'

Bill Taylor dashed into the casting bay. 'The – the doctor . . . he'll be here any minute . . .' He paused. 'Owen, for God's sake, man – what are you doing?'

He threw himself at Owen and caught him round the waist. 'Let him go, man alive . . . Let him go! D'you want to kill him?'

Two of the moulders sensed the danger. They tore Owen's hands away from the foreman's throat.

'Hell, man . . . What's come over you?' Bill Taylor panted. Owen pointed to the body of his friend.

'Ritchie's a goner,' he said slowly. 'And that swine's responsible.' He stared accusingly at the foreman.

Squint shuffled backwards into the safety of the crowd. 'Be – be careful what you say,' he stammered. He beckoned to the craneman.

'Dai! Lower the chain,' he called urgently. Then to Bill Taylor he shouted desperately: 'Take that box out to the yard, Bill. Break it up. We don't want no more trouble here after this accident.'

The crane rumbled forward. The chain was lowered and Bill Taylor and another moulder prepared to hitch the box.

'Just a minute, there!' Owen jumped to the box. He stood poised in front of it, his fists clenched. 'Take the crane away!' he shouted over his shoulder without glancing at the craneman.

'But, Owen,' Bill Taylor protested.

'You'll not touch this box.' Owen's face was grim. His eyes flashed and the knuckles of his hands showed white beneath the grime.

'Stand back!' he cried. 'My pal's been murdered. This box is the only evidence we have, and I'll see that a full report is made to doctor and police.'

Squint trembled like a man afflicted with the ague.

'The police!' he gasped. 'The police!'

He made an effort to regain his authority. 'You heard me, Bill Taylor!' he cried. 'Get that box out.'

Bill looked at Owen. One of the moulders approached him. 'I'll give you a hand, Bill.'

'Stand back!' Owen grabbed a heavy steel cramp and raised it shoulder high. 'I'll brain the first man that lays a hand on this box!'

The men glanced nervously at one another. Squint, desperate with fear, broke through to the front once more.

'Owen, for heaven's sake, be reasonable, man,' he pleaded. 'Think what this'll mean to me . . . My job . . . my livelihood. Hell, man – let's forget what I've said to you. Forget what I've said to Ritchie . . . I'll do anything . . . to compensate him.'

His words were unheeded. Owen stood guard between the smouldering box and the dead body of his friend. The men stood by as if transfixed.

And at that moment the doctor came.

Three Resolutions to One Kashmiri Encounter

AN ARID TITLE FOR A HUMAN INCIDENT

Giles Gordon

Giles Gordon, though a Scot, lives in London. He has published a number of novels and collections of short stories, and has also edited several collections. Like so many writers of short stories, Giles Gordon can see in a simple holiday incident, even if in something of an exotic setting, a way of exploring character. But whose character? This story has three different endings. Which of the three, do you think, really happened?

That morning I took a day tour in what was described in the brochure as a luxury coach from Srinagar – 'the russet-coloured, autumnal-smelling capital of Kashmir in the heady north of India' – to Gulmarg, 'the meadow of flowers', fifty-one kilometres away and 2,590 metres up in the Himalayas.

The coach from Srinagar, a ravishing city built on water, as colourful and chaotic as its name is impossible to pronounce, passed through lush countryside. On both sides of the straight, well-surfaced roads were paddy fields – many of them saturated with water, being worked on more often than not by women of all ages in floral pyjama outfits, the female national dress of Kashmir – and avenues of poplars. High up in the mountains was snow which, even in the last week of April, defied all efforts by the blazing sun to dislodge it. From the distance, the white on the peaks looked glossy and sleek like the coats of well-tended ponies.

We stopped for a ten-minute break at Tangmarg, a mountain village and another beauty spot five and a half kilometres from the higher Gulmarg. I suspect the coach and its driver required a breather before undertaking the final ascent, the road from Tangmarg being narrow, circuitous and hazardous. I say 'final ascent' –

final, that is, for vehicles, after which ponies and sledges, rope-tow and chair lift take over. The ski lifts were not in use, as on the lower slopes the snow had been melting for a couple of weeks, causing the rivers and streams to pour their brown and grey waters in torrents through the Kashmir valley. I didn't, at Tangmarg, avail myself of a cup of tea or coffee, as passengers were invited to do and most of the Indian families and couples did, preferring to wander up and down the single street of the village, looking at the bazaar and what through their open fronts the shops and stalls had to offer, and observe the mountain people. They were slim and wiry, taller and less stocky than the Nepalese, their faces without any spare flesh, tough, sun-beaten, snow-beaten: the countenance of a mountain people in the heart of Asia, further north than Tibet. They looked more Oriental than Indian. Visitors – five or six other coaches were parked in front of the Tourist Reception building in the middle of the village – mingled with the villagers. There was a whirl of activity. It was suddenly as if Tangmarg were a melting pot, the centre of the world. A stage had been animated.

A middle-aged man, with some distinction in his features and a dignified manner, was standing beside me, speaking to me. They tread so softly, so used are they to the terrain and the mountains, that you don't hear them approach. In good English – not at all with an Indian accent – he asked if I wouldn't prefer to leave the coach here and rejoin it on its return journey in the late afternoon, and he would guide me up the mountains, or wherever in the area I would like to go. I thanked him for his offer but declined.

'Only for six miles,' he said, and I was quietly pleased that he'd implied as great a mileage as that as being a short trek. He must have assumed I was more fit than I felt. The air up here made me tire easily and frequently search for breath. Again I declined, shaking my head.

'Let me come with you anyway,' he said, all the while absolutely and without difficulty managing to retain his character, individuality, dignity. There are beggars and beggars in India, indeed at times it seems both that they dominate the country and that the country has its being to enable them to beg, but not here in the exhilarating mountain air of Kashmir, gateway to heaven. There was, in this man, no element of grovelling, hardly even of importuning. He was his own master. His proposal was made entirely for my good. If I turned him down I was the loser.

'No, I prefer to go on my own,' I said. 'I'm sorry.' He seemed to accept my decision but showed no sign of being about to walk away, to solicit some other travellers. He began to tell me the names and heights of the local mountains, pointing them out to me, taking his time both as if to ensure I would manage to retain the information in my head and to prolong our encounter for its own sake. Besides, the *mountains* were hardly in a hurry. Harmukh and Ferozepur, Sunset Peaks and Apharwat Ridge. He kept the name and height of the last mountain, the mightiest of them all, to the end, producing it as if he'd just created the thing and I was the first to learn of his triumph: Nanga Parbat, 26,660 feet. How could I respond? Is *that* Nanga Parbat? Some height.

I said nothing, just looked. Still he stood by me, though it was as if I stood by him, as if I had sought him out and insisted on being with him. Somehow I felt it impossible – too discourteous to a fellow human being – to walk away from him. Besides, he might have followed me, though I didn't believe he would have done. And where could I have gone? Only up or down the village street, the street that was his village, his home. In my mind I urged the coach driver to sound his horn to indicate that we should all return to the vehicle, that it was about to move off and on to Gulmarg.

In a still, quiet voice – as if he was confiding in me – he began to talk again. 'Last year my wife died and I was left to bring up our three children. For six months one of them was in hospital, with a badly injured leg.' He paused, before going on. 'There is hardly any work here, in Tangmarg.'

I felt unable to say anything; or, rather, anything I might have said could only sound gratuitous, insensitive. He then said, so I understood it, that one rice meal a day for four people – and the children had big appetites – cost one rupee, which I'd have thought a little on the high side (a few pence) but hardly began to invalidate the point he was making. No work, no money, no food.

The horn of the coach went and I excused myself from him, saying that I hoped things got better for him, and quickly. I looked him in the eyes and nodded solemnly, as if to make it plain – in spite of having failed to provide him with employment and a rupee or two – that I wished him well. As if he could care. Somehow he managed neither to accept nor acknowledge my farewell, my intended affirmation of good will in the face of the facts, nor to reject it. He allowed me to go.

Inside myself, I had panicked – for the sake of a coin or two – and felt disgusted. I was filled with a fluttering self-loathing. As the coach moved away, I watched him walking slowly down the street, his body built for survival, his head lowered a little in the direction of the ground.

Six hours later the coach returned. I'd prayed that it wouldn't halt at Tangmarg but it did, as in the morning on the way up. During the day, walking miles in the relentless and joyous air of the mountains, I found that my encounter with the man at Tangmarg kept coming back to me, nagged and fretted at the edges of my mind. Because I hadn't provided him with work, even for a short period of time, an hour or two, he had no money and therefore couldn't buy rice for his children and himself. On the other hand, so I tried to rationalize, I was hardly the only person he could have asked. There had been thirty or forty coaches at Gulmarg, and they all must have stopped at Tangmarg in the morning on the upward climb. I didn't owe the man a living, or no more than anyone else did. I wasn't his keeper. Our encounter had been a chance one. Why then should I have felt so strongly that I was the only person he asked, that because of that I was responsible for his well-being and that of his family? Had he not an obligation to go on asking people if they'd like to use his services until someone responded in the affirmative?

I remained in the overheated and airless coach at Tangmarg on the way back because I could see him from where the vehicle was parked, sitting on the ground in front of a shop, his hands wrapped around his raised knees. He didn't seem to belong to the shop, either to be working there or to be purchasing something from it. How could he have done, if he'd no money? Yet he seemed aware of the conversation going on between the man behind the counter and the person he was chatting to on the other side, in the street.

He looked no more hopeful or dejected than he had in the morning. It was as if the day had passed him by. He may have noticed my coach, realized that it was the one I arrived on in the morning, but he gave no indication of looking or of seeing, of being interested or concerned. Besides, most of these coaches looked pretty alike. He had troubled my mind but I doubted whether I had his, that my rejection of his services and of him had remained with him for longer than the moment of rejection had taken. The irony, of course, was that it was he who had wanted, needed something from me, not me from him.

Ten minutes later the coach started up, began to move from its parking place and down the hill on the last stage of its journey back to Srinagar. For as long as he was in view I watched from behind the curtain of my window seat. He didn't look up.

Six hours later, when the sun was beginning to descend towards and behind the mountains and what had been the excited, frenetic atmosphere of Gulmarg was growing wistful, contemplative, the coach began its return journey. As in the morning, on the way out, it stopped at Tangmarg. During the bright and crisp and peaceful hours of day, up above the valley, watching the men of the mountains pull visitors on sledges up snowy slopes and in and out of fir and pine forests, my meeting of the morning with the would-be guide of Tangmarg kept coming back to me, worrying at my mind. Especially did it do so when I was eating a skilfully cooked egg *paratha* and drinking a cup of steaming black tea at a refreshment hut high up in the mountains. It was an image, the meeting between us, which I couldn't with a clear conscience – with any conscience at all – expel from my mind. Had the man been sycophantically crawling, simply for alms (*baksheesh*, a tip or reward) as is the case with the majority of the beggars of India, then I would have had no compunction in not slipping him a coin. After all, he was able-bodied and thus able to work – eager to work. Both, I suspected, for the satisfaction of the work itself and for the income it would bring him. To have given him a rupee or two would have made no noticeable difference to my pocket. To him and his dependants it would have meant sustenance for a day or even two.

I alighted from the coach at Tangmarg with the other passengers but I didn't filter slowly into the café or to one of the tea stalls as most of them did. I looked about for my man, the man of the morning, having decided before arriving back that if he was in the street

paratha: an Indian unleavened bread used with various fillings

and I saw him I would give him two rupees. One which I should have given him in the morning, the other to appease my conscience.

I saw him almost as soon as I had stepped from the coach, coming up the street, in nearly the same place he'd been in the morning when I saw him go down when the coach left. He wasn't looking up, he wasn't particularly looking up. He didn't give the impression of expecting to see someone he knew. Yet there was a kind of purposefulness about his progress, as if he wasn't proceeding up the street just to pass the time, to do something, that he wasn't walking merely for the sake of walking but that he had an objective in mind.

Though he was only a few paces from me, I began to move towards him. He looked up when I was close to him, three or four paces away, when he realized that someone was in his path. His eyes, which were both observant and bright yet somehow defeated, reconciled to the sorrows of life, of his life, registered no particular recognition of me; but neither the opposite. Our eyes met. I was neither stranger nor friend, enemy or ally.

'I wanted to thank you,' I said, 'for what you told me this morning.' The expression on his face didn't alter. 'About the mountains. Their names. Heights. Very interesting.'

I stopped. What more could I say, confronted with his silence, his lack of communication? I'd imagined he'd say something but he didn't. What could there have been for him to say? Yet he didn't seem to be judging me, despising me, which made it more difficult.

I held out my hand to him. His was raised to meet mine, to take the money. Without looking down to see how much it was, he took the note, then withdrew his hand.

'Thank you,' he said; and then once more, as if he wasn't sure that he'd uttered the words the first time. There was a slow, grateful nod of the head before he broke away and walked around me and continued up the street to wherever he'd been going.

Six hours later, by the time the coach began its return journey to Srinagar, I had resolved upon a course of action. The day, for me, had been an unusually satisfying one. Unusually so, because I'm not regularly given to wandering about the snow-covered Himalayas. I'd had no preconceptions as to how I'd feel up there, higher than I'd ever been, how free and irresponsible yet somehow in command of my destiny. Close to, with the sun grinning down on their great flanks, the mountains looked as if hewn from marble. The local men, wearing multi-coloured knitted caps and woollen jumpers, dragged docile Indians on holiday up the slopes on sledges, into and amidst forests of vast firs. Children and sometimes adults pelted each other laboriously with snowballs, at times giggling solemnly as if Indians shouldn't indulge themselves as abandonedly as this. A red-turbaned Sikh thundered along a path on a white pony, followed at a proper distance by his wife and two daughters on grey ponies. On the lower levels the snow was melting fast, as if a whole winter's downpour felt obliged to vacate itself in one afternoon when confronted by incipient spring. Water flooded down springy, grassy fields translating them into water meadows. Huge black crows cackled and cawed, glided from tree to snow, snow to tree, black against white.

Against this heightened atmosphere – in both senses, every sense – my unproductive (from his point of view) meeting with the man at Tangmarg in the morning lay at the back of my mind, tingeing my exultation in the present with irritation and dissatisfaction. Had the man begged, asked for alms, would I have given? After he'd told me his tale, assuming it was the same tale, I suspect I would. Not that, needing every coin and note and travellers' cheque I had with me in India, I'm in the habit of giving to beggars but because I believed the man implicitly, respected his self-respect and was grateful *not* to have him accompany me. I would have paid him so that I could be alone. All this, as I say, had he begged and importuned. But he didn't, he asked only to accompany me, to be my guide or companion for a period.

Near the end of the afternoon, before it was time to return to the coach, I had something tasty to eat and a glass of coffee with goat's milk at a café high up above the chair-lift wires. I took pleasure in watching the steam from the coffee rise upwards and look quite dark, almost opaque against the snow before turning translucent again and evaporating. Lurching downwards on the chair lift – above snow, trees, torrents of water, birds, people – I resolved what to do if the coach stopped at Tangmarg, as I felt pretty certain it would as Indians like their stops for tea or coffee. I even felt pleased with myself in anticipation.

As the coach parked in the centre of the village, the same spot as in the morning, alongside three other returning coaches, and with both villagers and visitors milling about, though without the excited tension, the expectancy of the morning, I at once saw my man. He was standing by a stall, a shop slightly down the sloping street from where the coach was. I hoped he wouldn't disappear before I could get out of the vehicle but, sitting near the back as I was, I was obliged to let the people in front alight first.

He was in the same place when I stepped out. I hurried over to him and stood there, smiling.

'Hallo,' I said.

'Sir,' he said, rather stiffly; 'sir', rather than the more usual 'sahib'.

I felt slightly hurt that he wasn't immediately more forthcoming, more friendly. *Presumably* he recognized me, remembered.

'Look,' I said, 'I'd like you to have this,' and held out to him the five-rupee note which I'd been clutching in my hand for half an hour or more. He looked down at it.

'No, sir,' he said, peering into my eyes. 'I asked you this morning if you'd employ me, and you wouldn't.' Then, without a pause: 'How did you like Gulmarg?'

'I . . . liked it . . . a lot,' I said, well aware of the feebleness of my response in the face of his rejection of my money, and of me.

'Yes, it is very beautiful,' he said.

'Very beautiful,' I repeated.

He walked away, up the street. Slowly I returned to the coach, crushing the note in my hand. There was little point in hurrying as the vehicle wouldn't be leaving until everyone had had their tea or coffee.

Thucydides

Rachel Gould

It is a seventeen-year-old talking. So it seems rather chatty. We are to have everything explained. She wants to be a writer. But then, she says quite early on: 'Like Thucydides, I shall leave something out. It's always more interesting, don't you think, when a writer leaves something out?'

Rachel Gould is a young journalist. She has worked for *Vogue* and contributed to *The Times* and the *Guardian*. She is now making a name for herself as a writer of short stories.

I expect you'd have mitched off school if you'd have been doing Thucydides. You thought nobody did Greek any more, I suppose? Well, when I was doing my A-levels, some people still did: two of us, to be precise, and Thucydides was what we started on. I don't know how much you know about Thucydides. I had a love-hate relationship with him (that's a cliché, I know, and perhaps I'll cut it out later, but at the moment I'm just trying to tell you the story). The Penguin translation I was using as a crib had something in the introduction about his style being obscure. He certainly was hellishly difficult at times. If he'd been alive today, he'd have been the sort of man – an academic probably – who speaks in inordinately long sentences, and who forgets half-way through quite what the structure of his sentence is, so that it ends in a way which is totally contradictory to the beginning. All very well, you might think? Yes, but he wasn't speaking, he was writing, so why didn't he correct himself afterwards? I never quite figured it out.

But on the other hand he was a fascinating man. I don't know whether you've seen Edward VI's diary in the British Museum, the one who was Elizabeth's brother – I think he was sixteen when he

A-level: in English schools, the examination that is taken after the age of sixteen. Students usually study three or four subjects over a two-year course. The storyteller here is, therefore, in her first of these two years and takes the exam at the end of her second year

died? Well, it's full of figures, statistics I mean: lists of all the cargoes coming into London with all the details of the number of barrels of salt fish and ballast and the tonnage of each vessel. He obviously had a passion for detail. I'm telling you this because Thucydides was the same. When you read about the battles in his War, you always knew how many people were on each side, how many were cavalry and how many hoplites, and what sort of shields they had, so you could have made a film about it, there was so much information. If he could find out the exact details from people who were in the battle, he gave them to you. And if he couldn't find out exactly, he made them up, so they would fit in. I don't think that matters, do you? (Some people did. They said this was history, and history shouldn't be made up. But I had a good answer to that: that the Greek for history is the same as the Greek for story, which is true.) And then, if you're a girl – I am, and I never wanted to be – it's useful to find out how you stake a harbour-bottom to sabotage an incoming enemy fleet, and things of that sort. I became very interested in military tactics. Thucydides was a general himself at the beginning of the war, so you know he gets things right. Later on he was disgraced in some strange way which he never makes clear, and was exiled from Athens – that's one of the few details he doesn't give you.

So that's why I liked and didn't like Thucydides.

I don't think the problems started in my first A-level year. I worked very hard – of course I was doing other subjects as well as Greek. In the evenings after I came back from school we had tea and watched some television and then I went up to my room. I don't remember working on my other subjects, but I remember Thucydides. I had my book case on my left, opposite the bed, and my desk – only a table, really – next to that, with my volume of Thucydides and a vocabulary book and the two huge volumes of the Liddell and Scott dictionary. I worked slowly. At the beginning I was prepared to gloss over difficulties. I knew there was a lot I didn't *really* understand, and my vocabulary was small, and sometimes I had to look up almost every word in a sentence. But as I got better, I became more perfectionist. I would worry over a sentence for minutes, half an hour perhaps, until I not only understood the gist

hoplite: a Greek infantryman. Thucydides was the historian of the Greeks and their war against the Persian Empire

of what he was saying, but the relationship, grammatically, of every word to every other word in the sentence. And that was difficult, because Thucydides was so obscure, as I said before. Sometimes my father offered to help me, but I refused. He taught classics at the University, he was clever and a patient teacher, but I wanted to convince myself that I could cope with Greek on my own, without help.

So that was how the first year went. It was in the second year that things started going wrong. Not right at the beginning of the year, I think, but after a time I'd got myself into a hell of a mess. I had boy problems too, but I won't go into details over that. Like Thucydides I shall leave something out. It's always more interesting, don't you think, when a writer leaves something out? You can mull it over and wonder, and then it gives the critics a chance to have their different interpretations. Anyway, somehow I stopped working. It happened like this. One day, I hadn't had time to prepare any Greek. I felt guilty, and I didn't go to my class. Then the next class, I felt even guiltier – not only had I not prepared my Greek, but I hadn't gone to the previous class, and those two things together were harder to explain than either of them separately. So I didn't go to that class either. And so it went on, until it had escalated to such a point that I had to avoid my classics teacher in the school assembly hall, in the corridors, everywhere. So then I had to mitch off school. Perhaps it's not called mitching where you live, but that's what it's called in Swansea. It means staying away from school without having a letter from your parents to say that you were ill, or had to go to the dentist, or were looking so pale that your mother thought you surely *would* be ill, if she insisted on your taking that horrid long bus journey. I just mitched.

Perhaps I should have mentioned before that I lived in Swansea, but it's not really central to the story. Suffice it to say that it's where Dylan Thomas went to school – you probably know that. But now I'd better give a brief description of where we lived, because that will explain a few things. You probably think that descriptions are boring. I do too, but you see, I want to be a writer later on, and writers always give descriptions at some point in the narrative, and so I think I should practise, and you'll have to bear with me.

Dylan Thomas: famous Swansea poet and story writer who died young. He had his problems!

When we came to Swansea, we looked at all sorts of different houses – old ones in the old parts, ones near the University and ones out beyond the Mumbles on Gower Peninsula, but what we chose was a hole in the ground. I mean that literally. By the time we came to move, the house was more or less finished, but when we first went to look at the site it was just a hole with a bulldozer in it amongst lots of other holes. So why did we choose it? Because of the view. If I were Tolstoy I could wax lyrical about that view. The house was almost at the brow of a hill which led on to a wild, marshy patch of common land where sometimes, in the very early morning, you saw foxes, and then to a golf course. The other way, towards the south, it looked over Swansea bay to the crooked Mumbles peninsula with its lighthouse and the coast of Devon beyond, and on the other side out towards the enormous Port Talbot oil refinery which grew plumes of smoke in the day time, and brilliant orange flames in the night, burning off the waste gases. It wasn't a view you would call sublime, I suppose, but it had something of everything, and it was never boring to look at. The sea was the best thing. In towns you tell the weather and the seasons by the greenness of plants and the times that flowers grow. But in Swansea you told the weather from the mood of the sea as well. The sea is more extreme. Sometimes an intense blueness with tiny foam-caps to each wave, but sometimes a thick angry oily grey, and enormous waves breaking over the sea wall at Mumbles and flooding the fishermen's cottages. I didn't realize how much I loved the sea until I left.

Then down the street and round the corner from the house was the park. It had been the grounds of a large house at the bottom of the park which now belonged to the University. It was a strange park, a bit fantastical. The people from the house must have had a good head-gardener, a man with a bizarre imagination. At the top, nearest our house, was an area of dogs' graves, about ten of them, all labelled with their names and dates, with daffodils and violets growing round them in the spring. Then there was a long wide sweep of grass that ran straight down the hill to the sea road. On one side was the big house, on the other a wood, and beyond that an area with a curious winding stream planted thickly with rhododendrons that grew luscious jungle flowers of red and white and dark pink. In one place there was a folly, and in another a sort of Chinese pagoda with a Chinese bridge crossing a pond covered with water lilies. Nothing could have been more incongruous in a park in Swansea, and it was one of my favourite places.

I said that this description was going to help you understand how things happened, and this is why. Every morning we walked through that park down the grass slope to the sea road where we waited for the bus to school. We is myself and my brothers and sister. I forgot to tell you until now that I had any brothers or sisters – it didn't seem necessary because this story is really about me, and a little about my father. But I just wanted you to know that I wasn't an only child, in case you thought in that ridiculous Freudian way that it was because I was an only child that I worked so hard and let the work get on top of me and then had to mitch off school. So usually we walked together and caught the bus together, but sometimes one or other of us went early, to play football before school started, or copy someone's homework if we hadn't had time to do it the night before, or it had been too difficult. When I got into this dreadful muddle at school it didn't seem odd to any of them that I started getting up a bit earlier and going off to catch an earlier bus. In fact, that isn't what I was doing. I walked down to the park gates, turned right just inside the fence and walked to the Chinese pagoda. If it was sunny I sat on the steps leading down to the pool, and if it was raining I sat inside the pagoda. Sometimes I spent the whole morning there reading. You mustn't think that I was lazy, and that that was why I mitched. It was just that Thucydides was so obscure. I said just now that I want to be a writer, and probably already then I had an idea that that was what I wanted to be, so I read voraciously, especially poetry. But if it was very cold, I couldn't bear a whole morning in the pagoda, and I timed on my watch, carefully, the times when everyone should have left the house – my brothers and sister to my school, my mother to the junior school where she taught, and my father to the University, plus half an hour for all eventualities (the car breaking down, or someone oversleeping). Then I went back up through the park to the house, let myself in and spent the rest of the day in comfort in my room.

Well, this is where we get to the main point of the story, where you will see how indirectly Thucydides was the cause of my discovering something awful. If he hadn't made his Peloponnesian War so difficult to read, I don't suppose I ever would have discovered, and if I hadn't discovered I probably would not have done a lot of things I did afterwards. Because the discovery made me change my views about a great many things. If you were going to be Freudian about things, you would probably say that it caused my transition from puberty to adulthood. And everyone knows how painful that transition is.

It was late spring by this time, but in Swansea the spring, instead of bringing the first fine weather and being the harbinger of summer, was often the beginning of a rainy season that I sometimes thought couldn't be much worse than the monsoons. As the alarm went off in the morning you were immediately aware of the constant sound of water, falling from the sky, pouring down the gutters and the drains and in streams down the road. The lawns in front and behind the house were water-logged, the trees sprouted moulds on their trunks, and in the park it was difficult to avoid the slugs there were so many. On this particular morning the rain was so heavy I considered not leaving the house at all, but that would have been dangerous, and I got myself up and to the park in the end.

I don't know why, but when I got back to the house, my father's car was still in the drive. Perhaps I hadn't allowed the full extra half an hour – it was so wet and I was so cold. The only thing to do was to wait in the garage until he left, and that's what I did. It was a case of making the best of a bad job. Some people's garages are so neat you could quite happily live in them, but ours wasn't one of those. The old book case of my grandfather's, with its jam-jars full of rusting nails and screws, tins of oil and coils of fuse-wire, was the neatest thing in it. The rest was a chaotic jumble – the lawn-mower and the step-ladder, tools and a flat tyre – and there was hardly enough light coming through the one low window to read by. So I simply sat, listening to the rushing rain, and through that for the scraping of the front door against the metal door-sill, which would signal my father's departure. After almost half an hour the rain seemed to ease off a little, and then the door scraped and I heard the clicking of my father's shoes – he had recently taken to wearing a pair of old-fashioned black lace-up shoes, with metal half-moons at the back of the heel to stop them wearing down. But then as I stood up and tried to rub the pins and needles out of my legs, I thought I heard other footsteps. I probably wouldn't have been sure – the rain was still swirling down the gutters – but then I heard voices. One was my father's; the other a woman's voice, not my mother's.

'Get in,' he said. 'I'll drive you to the bus-stop.'

'Couldn't you take me all the way? I've got a class at eleven and the weather's filthy.'

'Sorry. We might be seen. You really shouldn't have come here either. It was a stupid thing to do.'

'I had to. I was miserable after yesterday evening and I thought you might . . .'

Her voice trailed off, the doors slammed, and after some damp rumblings the engine started up and the car reversed up the drive and then down the hill. The quietness of the rain flowed slowly back and I stared blankly at the rust on the back of the garage door. I thought of my mother starting on the third lesson of the day on the other side of the town.

It was at the end of that week that the school telephoned my parents to tell them that I hadn't been to school for some weeks. I must have suspected that things were coming to a head. I had gone to bed with a slight temperature and the beginnings of a cold, a real one, but one which stemmed not so much from sitting in the damp garage as from my state of mind, which was as dismal as the weather. My parents came up separately to talk to me. My mother remonstrated quietly, and my father lectured me slightly. I cried. He thought I was crying about Thucydides, in repentance for the work I hadn't done. But I was crying about him. I was seeing things in a different perspective, and Thucydides didn't seem so much of a problem as he had before.

The Girl in the Mad Hat

Dorothy Goulden

When you have read this story, you may, perhaps, find yourself looking again at the title. There are other early warning signs too!

Dorothy Goulden works as a secretary at the University of Sussex and is married with a grown-up family. Her hobby is writing stories and plays.

Diana stood at the barrier and watched the train disappearing from view. Disconsolately she turned away. She had missed it by seconds and she hated being late for the office. Then she thought of the letter in her bag. It was from her son, Stephen. She had longed to open it before she left the house, but there was not time. Now she could read it over and over again in that long wait before the next train.

Hugging the thought to herself, she went over to the form opposite the barrier. A young girl, already sitting there, made room for her. Diana had a confused impression of gleaming spectacles and a moon-shaped, anxious face.

'I'm sorry,' said the girl. 'I do seem to take up a lot of room.'

A bulging plastic bag and a cartwheel hat lay between them on the seat. 'I don't want to crush your hat,' said Diana. She opened her bag and took out the letter.

'Dear Mother,' she read. 'I'm sorry to be so long in writing. As you see from the address, I have moved. I am on the fifth floor of this grotty house, but never mind . . .'

'I'll move this out of your way.' The girl picked up the plastic bag and deposited it on the floor.

'Don't worry,' murmured Diana.

'The landlord has promised to mend the roof. You must come for the weekend when I'm straight. There's a smashing view from here – you would love it.'

The girl's voice was soft and insistent. 'I thought I'd lost my ticket.'

Diana turned the page. 'I've heard nothing about that job I told you about. How are things with *you*?'

'But I found it in the bottom of my handbag. Do *you* ever do things like that?'

Diana looked up. 'Will you excuse me,' she said. 'I'm trying to read.'

The girl had great dark eyes behind the spectacles. She beamed happily at Diana and chatted on. 'I'm always losing things. When I go anywhere, I keep tight hold of my bag. If I don't, I leave it on the train or the bus.'

Diana looked at her watch. There were ten more minutes before the train. 'That's very sensible of you,' she said, and deliberately turned her shoulder.

'Have you thought any more about getting a car? I don't know how you stand that train journey.'

It was useless to read. The girl was shuffling her feet on the concrete floor. Diana stared down, hypnotized. They were large feet, encased in red sandals.

'Are you admiring my sandals?' The girl stuck her legs out stiffly in front of her – strong, sturdy legs, uncompromisingly plump.

'They're very pretty sandals,' said Diana gravely.

'My mum bought them for me last week. She said I needed a pair to go away with.'

She swung her feet up and down, admiring the sandals. Diana watched her. She had dark hair, cut short just below the ears and curving down from a centre parting. Her round face had a strange, two-dimensional effect; Diana suddenly remembered a rag doll she had been given as a child.

Beyond the barrier a train had just drawn in. Doors were opening, people alighting on the platform. Diana got up thankfully. 'I do believe this is my train,' she said, gathering up her bag and the precious letter.

'Are you going to Slindon Junction?' said the girl. 'Could I travel with you? Please?'

She stood up. Her cotton skirt stood out stiffly, away from her body. In one hand she held the cartwheel hat; a garish flower drooped raggedly over the brim. The plastic bag sagged from her other hand, almost touching the floor. She was a large girl and towered over Diana like a grotesque doll.

The people from the incoming train crowded through the barrier. Diana watched them disperse along the concourse; young girls, shining spruce in their chainstore clothes; women with powdered faces, avidly talking to each other; young men with non-committal eyes. She wanted to cry out for help, but they were work-a-day crowds. The unpredictable only happened at weekends at the touch of a button.

'Your bag is trailing on the floor,' she said sharply. The girl's eyes filled with tears. Diana looked away.

She waited until the last person cleared the barrier. The ticket collector nodded and waved her on as she produced her season ticket. Her heels clicked along the platform. Behind her the girl struggled and gasped, dropping her bag, showing the wrong ticket, rag doll face red with exertion.

'I ought to help her,' thought Diana. 'But I can't. It would give her a claim on me.'

The girl caught her up. 'I can't keep up with you. Are you sure you don't mind me travelling with you?'

Diana ignored this. 'Come on, we'll get in here. It's a non-smoker.'

It was an old-fashioned compartment with a corridor at one end and two long seats facing each other. Diana settled herself in a corner seat. The girl sat down opposite, her skirt bunched round her solid figure. The plastic bag bulged and splayed out on the seat beside her.

'Why don't you put your things on the rack?' said Diana. Then reluctantly, 'Here, let me help you.'

'Oh no, I mustn't do that.' The girl clutched the brim of her hat. 'I might leave them on the train. I told you. I do that sometimes. My mum gets ever so cross.'

Diana stared out of the window. It was almost time to go. There was a flurry of passengers, a slamming of doors and the guard blew his whistle. Too late, Diana realized that she and the girl were alone in the compartment. This ridiculous girl with her wet eyes and vapid face. She would tell Stephen about it. 'Oh, go on,' he would say. 'You're a soft touch.'

The train slid smoothly out of the station, past the sidings with their conglomeration of trucks and along the track that curved round to the viaduct.

'Where are you going?'

'I'm not telling you,' thought Diana. Aloud she said, 'I change trains at Slindon Junction.'

'I'm going to stay with my friend. I have to catch a bus when I leave the train.'

Diana gazed out at the view from the viaduct. Down below, row upon row of houses stretched away to the skyline. An arterial road cut through the patchwork of densely packed terraces. It was a familiar scene to Diana, but this morning every outline stood out sharply as if she had extra vision. She saw a group of people standing at a zebra crossing. The traffic waited and they crossed. Further along, the same traffic stopped at a set of traffic lights. Seen from the viaduct it was like a silent movie with the rhythm of the train making an accompaniment.

'My friend – you know, the friend I'm staying with – belongs to a funny religious sect. They all wear hats.'

Diana turned her head. 'I beg your pardon.'

'They all have to wear hats.' The girl's eyes shone with pleasure at Diana's incredulity.

'What, all of them?'

'No, not the men, just the women. I don't know what they are. Just a funny religious lot. They're strict about wearing hats. That's why I bought one.'

She poked at the artificial flower on the brim, pulling it to shreds.

'It's a very large brim,' said Diana. 'Do they wear hats all the time?'

The girl shook her head. 'No, only when they go out. But that's bad enough. It's a mad house, what with their hats and everything. The women aren't allowed to wear trousers, only dresses. My friend wants to wear jeans and go to discos. It's a shame. *My* mum doesn't mind what I wear.'

They had left the built-up area. The houses backing on to the railway line had gardens and proud new extensions. Diana saw a woman bending over a flower bed, watched by two small children.

The girl began to rummage through her plastic bag. It fell sideways on the seat, spilling out a pink brassière and a toilet bag. The cartwheel hat slid off her knee; Diana picked it up. The ribbon round the brim was black with grime.

'How long are you staying with your friend?' she said.

'I'm staying for two days.' The words came out in a rush. 'After that my boyfriend is coming to pick me up. He came to see me last night but I was out and when I got back he'd left, so my mum said I would be leaving my friends the day after tomorrow and that's why he's picking me up then.'

She stopped, breathless. Her eyes never left Diana's face.

'He's ever so nice. We've known each other since I was fourteen. We might get married. My parents won't mind – I don't think they will.'

Diana felt a great drowsiness. There were people talking in the next compartment but they sounded a long way off.

'You're very lucky,' she said mechanically, not caring.

The train rushed through Blatchington Halt. Through the window she saw a steep embankment, covered with lush foliage. 'Look at the flowering valerian. The roots of the plant make people sleepy and cats hysterical. Stephen is great on herbs, he told me.'

She thought she had said the words aloud, but the girl was still talking. 'My mum's ever so nice. She's got a shaggy perm and she wears pencil skirts. She dresses really young. Not like my friend's mum.'

The train rushed through a tunnel and for fifteen seconds Diana's ears were filled with a roaring sound. The girl watched her, eyes bright in the electric light. Then it was daylight and her voice came out of the roaring. 'My friend's mum is nice, ever so homely. She's got her hair in a sort of roll – my mum says she ought to do herself up a bit more – but she's nice, my friend's mum. She lets me put all my stuff in the bathroom when I stay with them. It's not her fault about the religious stuff and all that.'

'I never said it was,' said Diana.

'It's my friend's dad, he's very strict.'

'I'm getting out soon,' said Diana.

There was a burst of laughter from the next compartment.

'The people next door are laughing at us,' said the girl.

'No, they're not,' said Diana, sitting up straight and reaching for her bag. 'Now, look, you're trailing your hat ribbon on the floor.'

'They're laughing at us. They're laughing at you as well as me.' The girl made no attempt to wipe away the tears rolling down her cheeks.

There was a great hurrying and commotion as the train drew in at Slindon Junction. Diana got up to open the carriage door, then hesitated.

'Nobody is laughing at us,' she said. 'I must leave you now. I'm late.'

'Don't go. Please – please –' The girl gripped her arm and pulled her back from the door. People stood about on the platform; a voice over the tannoy announced the departure of the train; no one got into the compartment. Diana struggled to free herself, but she was in a grip of steel. 'Let go, you great – stupid lump – let go of my arm –'

In one movement the girl turned her round and pushed her down the seat. The force behind the push made Diana gasp. 'You stupid girl,' she said weakly. 'I'll be carried on to – the next station. Oh, you stupid girl.'

The train slid out of the junction and along the glittering tracks that lay beyond. The girl put her hands on Diana's shoulders, pressing her down on the seat.

'You called me stupid. And I thought you were my friend. I thought you were ever so nice. Even when you wanted to read your silly letter.'

Diana stared up at the wet dark eyes behind the spectacles. She started to cry.

The Other Launderette

Helen Harris

A number of stories by Helen Harris have appeared in magazines. Though she now lives in London, she did live in France for a good many years and so knows well the background to this story. The 'I' of the story is a man; presumably the woman running the launderette is French. Then there are the 'Arabs' – probably from Algeria, for very large numbers of Algerians have come to France for work and they suffer as ethnic minorities so commonly do in Europe. At the start, the reader may be worried by the attitudes expressed by the narrator and the woman. But wait until the end! So much depends on the eyes through which Helen Harris is asking us to look.

Going to the launderette in the Place des Innocents was almost fun. I had switched my allegiance from a grubby little six-machine establishment at the end of the street when I found out that at the Place des Innocents there were nearly current issues of *Paris Match* and *Jours de France* and the woman who minded the washing-machines was svelte and soignée. The caretaker at the other launderette was, I am afraid to say, a most gruesome hag. No, not a hag, maybe; more a harpy, for she exuded a definitely lewd quality, despite her hideous appearance. A mat of dark, long hair flapped around her bloated face. She had mottled, swollen cheeks, which she sucked in and out obsessively. Her eyes flickered under thick, raw lids, which you could imagine being sold by weight in a charcuterie. She wore consistently a giant brown knitted cardigan over an old, flowery dress and, possibly most horribly of all, a pair of grubby, flirtatious little slippers, which seemed a mockery of her distended feet.

She called me, 'Meestur'. My first visit to the launderette ought

Paris Match, Jours de France: illustrated weekly magazines
svelte: slim
soignée: smart
charcuterie: a French shop selling cooked meats and a variety of sausages

really to have been my last. But, in a silly way, one relishes these sordid experiences abroad, which one would not tolerate at home. I came in with my great bag of dirty washing and my accent, as I asked for a cup of detergent, informed her straight away that she had an Englishman on her hands. 'Ah Meestur,' she cried warmly, bustling forward. She sized up my recent haircut and reasonably good jacket and then waddled into her cubby-hole at the back to fetch the detergent. She stood over me as I loaded a machine, perhaps intentionally the one nearest the door, and seemed full of curiosity about my clothes. I was rather embarrassed. I had spent most of the last month settling down in the city and certainly hadn't given much thought before then to washing my clothes. They were pretty distasteful. But the caretaker did not seem concerned by all the grey collars and dubious socks. She bent forward and examined them frankly. 'What kind of collars are those?' she asked. 'That pullover, is it Shetland?' I bundled my things in as fast as I could and tried to hide the underpants inside the shirts. But my reticence did not discourage her and in her eagerness to see properly, she craned even closer. Then I noticed that she was none too fresh herself.

I sat down to wait and opened my book. Behind me, the caretaker had a mystifying conversation with another customer about her life. 'There are days,' I heard her say in an addled voice, 'when I wonder how I cope with it all, really I do. It's more than a normal person can bear. What with Their foreign coins jamming up the machines and flooding and now a whole house of Them opposite to cap it all, sometimes, honestly, I just wish it would end.'

When my machine finished, she was at the ready, with a plastic basket to transfer the clothes to a dryer. I took it from her rather promptly and protested, 'Non, non, madame, let me.' I tried to imply that I was doing it out of politeness but, of course, it was to avoid her fingers pawing my clothes. She beamed all over at being treated with such respect.

I cannot remember exactly when I came back for the second time. I am not all that keen on washing so let's say it was three or four weeks later. It would have been in the evening because the place was very full and I remember feeling relieved that the caretaker's attentions would be generally shared. The other customers were mainly Arabs, skinny, moustached labourers, staring mournfully at the turning drums. The air was blue with cheap cigarette smoke.

The harpy was behaving atrociously. Through the steam and cigarette smoke, she was bellowing, apparently at no one in particular, 'Vile, that's what it is, vile. Maybe it's all right to carry on like that in some countries, but don't you dare try it here.' I couldn't quite understand what the matter was, but I assumed that someone had unhygienically broken some regulation of the launderette.

The woman was quite immense in her fury. Every now and then, she would make an angry rush at one of the small men and almost jostle him, crying, 'Oh yes, go on, sit there, pretend it's nothing to do with you. You don't fool me, Mohammed, I know you're all the same.'

I put my clothes in as fast as possible and went out to walk around the evening. When I came back half an hour later, the launderette had cleared and the caretaker's rage seemed to have focused on one man. He was sitting rigidly straight at the end of the bench, self-righteously watching his clothes bump round and round in the suds, while, above him, the crazed figure hissed and squawked. She turned to me as I came in and cried, 'Ah, Meestur, tell this wretch how gentlemen behave in your country. They have such filthy habits where he comes from.' The Arab barely moved his head in my direction. He had clearly decided to submit to this persecution in silence, for the sake of clean clothes. I admired his tenacity.

'It's cold outside, isn't it?' I said rather feebly and burrowed into the dank drum to extract my washing. Behind me, the enraged caretaker gave a harsh laugh.

Then I came again in the daytime, on my day off. I had a newspaper, which I intended to hold up in front of my face, if necessary, like a screen. But the place was shut. An impromptu paper notice on the door said 'Closed Hour Due Circumstances'. I was walking back down the street, feeling displeased, when I heard a shriek behind me. I turned round to see the launderette woman, arms flailing extravagantly, beckoning to me from a café doorway. She called, 'It's all right, Meestur. We're opening right away. It's fine for you.' I hesitated. She darted back into the café and reappeared with a half-full glass of porto. She bobbed it at me explanatorily and then patted her cardigan pocket where, presumably, she kept her keys. Oh well, I thought limply, I'll get the chore over with. I started to go reluctantly back towards the launderette; I did not relish the prospect of half an hour's intimacy with the harpy. When I reached the café doorway, she cackled placatingly and, to my dismay, actually suggested I came in for a drink too. 'I'm in a hurry,' I said rather brusquely, 'I haven't got time.' 'Ah bon, ah bon,' the woman said good-humouredly and, causing me slight guilt, she downed her glass, returned it to the bar and came hobbling up the street with me to her launderette.

That time, I came close to abandoning the horrid place. In the steamy gloom – she did not bother to switch on all the lights just for me – there was a melancholic atmosphere, which provoked the miserable woman to confide in me. (Was that glass of porto her first?) She sat down beside me on the long bench and, for a minute, just watched my clothes turn sympathetically, as if they were whimsical fish frolicking in an aquarium. 'They're pretty, aren't they?' she said, 'all those sleeves hugging each other.'

'Well now, I'd better do my shopping,' I said and she placed her hand, briefly, on my knee.

'You cook for yourself, do you?' she asked tenderly. 'Dinner for one?'

My life in the city had never struck me as pathetic till then; I rather enjoyed the ritual of cooking on my single gas ring, going down to the market to choose fruit and cheese. But there was something so ghastly behind her maudlin inquiry that I suddenly felt desperate. I had a vision of myself eating a meal on my own, all off the one plate, with a book in front of me, that horrified me by its nightmarish solitude.

'It's not always easy on one's own, is it?' she went on, 'I know all about it, believe me. I've been through it all since my husband died.'

'Yes,' I said, standing up, 'I have to buy some dinner.' I added brutally, 'I've invited friends.'

I came back half an hour later with a loaded bag of groceries. I had missed the moment to unload my clothes and they were already rotating in the dryer. The caretaker welcomed me back with approval. 'You're a good boy,' she said primly, 'you keep your clothes nice and clean, I see.'

I blenched, but she did not seem inclined to continue the theme. She was smoking, with one elbow propped on a washing-machine, and she appeared uncharacteristically placid. I topped up the dryer with one-franc pieces and opened my paper. Behind me, the woman stubbed out her cigarette with a nasty grinding noise and began on some launderette job. There was a fair bit of dragging and sighing, which I resolutely ignored. Then she appeared momentously in front of me with an armful of dirty washing. 'You keep your clothes nice and clean,' she repeated, unfolding her bundle, 'Not like some people.' And, to my utter disgust, she started to display the inner crevices of the clothes, dismally encrusted with filth and grime. 'Sickening,' she said. 'Isn't it? Vile.'

I could only stammer, 'Who – whose are they?'

She swelled triumphantly as she said, 'Theirs. They're all as bad as each other when it comes to cleanliness, you know, those Arabs.'

After this, needless to say, I more than dreaded the place. I did go again, once or twice, before the dénouement, but nothing memorable happened. Visits to the launderette hardly constitute events in the normal course of affairs. I was leading a full, rich life in the city and I certainly didn't look to the launderette for any sleazy thrill.

Then, about six months ago, I went there for the last time. The woman wasn't in the launderette, but the door was open when I arrived so I went in and put my clothes in to wash. It was a relief to find the place empty. I sat down in front of my machine, lit a cigarette and stretched my legs. After maybe ten minutes, I noticed a lopsided couple approaching along the opposite side of the street; a teetering female balloon and a minute male. It was not until they were nearly opposite and turning to cross the road that I actually registered what my vision held. It was the caretaker, arm in arm with one of the Arabs. I stayed rooted to the bench, unable to react for surprise and shock. They crossed the street and came up to the door of the launderette. To my amazement, I recognized the little man whom the harpy had abused so viciously in the launderette that night a few months previously. They came in cosily and we said 'Bonjour.' The woman looked pink and very pleased with herself, her little slippers clopped on the tiles. I had stood up, expecting some sort of confrontation, but she seemed quite unembarrassed by my presence.

'Bonjour Meestur,' she trilled, 'All O.K. with the machine? No problems?' The Arab eyed me sullenly and I answered brightly, 'Oh no, oh no. I think it's almost finished.' They went through into the little cubby-hole at the back and then the woman came out again with a scrap of paper in her hand. She grinned at me unspeakably and up went that tatty sign again, 'Closed Hour Due Circumstances'.

I hurried to finish. I was overcome with such revulsion for the place, I could hardly wait to leave it. I was a naïve idiot, I told myself; if ever there was a den of vice, this was it. The caretaker treated me like a regular. She padded cosily around her establishment, letting down the Venetian blinds, turning out the lights, until I felt I was becoming involved in their foul act. She even asked me to join them for an aperitif.

I banged the glass door behind me and, having found a better launderette, I never went back. There had been preliminary giggles from the cubby-hole as I fumed in front of the dryer and, twice, the small Arab had come out and glared at me.

I felt resentful. That revelation had shown me that, in certain respects, I was still a callow English public schoolboy, with stale socks. I loathed the place which had proved it and, in what is, I suppose, a classic act of revenge, I decided to write about it. In time, my indignation was moderated by pity. What a wretched, debased world they inhabited.

The smart supervisor and the magazines at the Place des Innocents were all very fine. But I could not help feeling sometimes, as I sat under the blown-up photographs of Alpine meadows, that I was dodging the issue by coming here and that the other launderette was real life.

Trust Mother Audry

Thomas Hinde

Thomas Hinde is an established novelist, author of some sixteen books. He has also written books on travel, history and gardening. He is a regular reviewer too.

This story is set in a convent – a closed community – not unlike a boarding-school perhaps! Or a family? Certainly, living closely together brings out our strengths and weaknesses – and strong feelings!

They went out with Mother Audry to cut down the old tree: Sister Agatha, Sister Teresa, Sister Paula and Sister Martha. Sister Martha was the youngest.

The tree was an elm which had got the disease – it was a mercy, Mother Audry said, because it had always stood in the wrong place, making the chapel dark and gloomy, when it should be full of light. Sister Martha knew that Mother Audry would never have cut it down if it was alive.

Since they depended on wood for heating, it was twice a mercy. Wood had become terribly expensive, Mother Audry said. It might have been a mistake to buy the wood stove. Oh no, Sister Martha wanted to cry out, though she loved Mother Audry's honesty. We must pray for help, Mother Audry said. And, lo and behold, a couple of weeks later she had found that the old elm tree had died. It was as if God, seeing their need – and knowing it was in the wrong place – had decided to kill two birds with one stone. It was a kind of miracle, though when Martha had suggested this, Mother Audry had told her not to be silly, child.

The rebuke had made Sister Martha a little faint with joyful humility.

Three times a mercy, in fact, because the tree leaned away from the chapel so there was no need to employ a firm of tree surgeons, whose absurd price, Mother Audry explained, would have exceeded the value of the firewood. So instead she had borrowed an electric chain saw from the farm – not worrying them by saying why she wanted it. Watching that saw which she carried now in her strong left hand, Sister Martha's heart beat fast with admiration. Given the chance she knew she would die for Mother Audry, though the thought alarmed her since it was surely for God that she should be ready to die, and she didn't feel the same enthusiasm for that idea.

As they went, Sister Agatha paid out the cable for the saw. She carried the coil in her left hand and paid it out with her right, and kept getting it caught up in her habit. Once when she bent to disentangle it she managed to knock her rimless glasses off her nose. Sister Martha wanted to giggle.

Sister Teresa carried a big iron wedge. She was tall and thin, with a pale oval face. She carried the wedge in her long pale hands in front of her chest, like an offering. Beyond her wimple her lips moved. She was praying.

Sister Paula carried a hammer with a long handle. She was almost as young as Sister Martha, but had a fat red face with spots. As soon as some faded, more would erupt. She carried the hammer in one fat red hand, which the scrubbing water made redder in this cold weather. It was, of course, because of her red hands and spots that Mother Audry had given her this responsible job. It was wrong of Sister Martha to hope the hammer would not be needed, but there was something she could not bear about the smug way Sister Paula carried it in her horrible red hand, while she herself had nothing to carry.

She couldn't even pray, like Sister Teresa, she was far too excited. This big tree coming crashing down. Mother Audry, with the blue saw in one strong hand and over her other shoulder a coil of rope – the tree leaned in the right direction, it was true, but the rope was to make sure. Though how they would tie it to the tree, Sister Martha could not imagine. Even Mother Audry could hardly climb up and tie it, dressed as she was.

She shouldn't have doubted. Mother Audry had also brought a ball of string. As soon as they stopped on the squelchy lawn and put down their things, those of them who had any, she produced it from a fold in her habit. One end she tied to a piece of brick, then let each

habit: the traditional dress of a nun
wimple: a piece of cloth, worn by nuns, covering the head, neck and chin

of them try to throw this over one of the tree's branches. When Sister Agatha threw, it turned out she was treading on the rest of the string and the brick came back and hit her on the shin. Sister Martha could see that behind her glasses she was crying with pain and rage. Fancy an old woman like that crying over such a thing. Sister Martha thought of Sister Agatha as an old woman, though she'd been told she was only forty-three.

Sister Martha tried next, but the brick only made a silly loop in the air then bounced along the path in front of them. When Sister Paula tried, she didn't throw at all but pushed it with her red hand and stumpy arm. It went an even shorter way.

'Well done, Paula,' Mother Audry said.

Sister Teresa tried next, and the brick went high, but unfortunately the string wasn't tied to it. As she watched someone else retrieve it her lips moved faster.

Then Mother Audry tried. She didn't throw it but bowled it. High up it went, over a branch on a level with the chapel's gutter, then came sploshing down onto the grass. When Mother Audry bowled the brick, her arms and legs spread out, she looked for a moment as if she was being crucified. Not the way Our Lord was, Sister Martha thought, but like St Patrick – who asked to be done diagonally, the same as the cross on his flag, so that he'd be different. Or was that St Andrew?

'Oh Mother!' Sister Paula exclaimed, in false amazement, because *of course* Mother Audry would be the one to succeed. Well that wouldn't do Sister Paula any good. The one thing Mother Audry hated was hypocrisy. She was good at detecting it, too. Now, when she smiled at Sister Paula it was with pity that she could be so false.

Mother Audry took the string from the brick and tied it to the end of the rope, then used the string to pull the rope over the branch. Next she tied the end of the rope in a slip knot round its other dangling side and pulled so that the slip knot went up tight against the branch. How helpless she made the rest of them seem.

Just as she finished, the icy wind came round the end of the chapel, catching their habits and blowing Sister Paula's so high she showed one fat red knee. Now Sister Martha did laugh, though she managed to put her hand to her mouth and turn it into a cough. The wind hardly moved the old tree. It stood there without leaves, tall and still, almost as if it knew what was going to happen to it. When

Sister Martha looked up to its highest branches against the grey sky she felt giddy. There was something so sullen about it that just for an instant she wondered whether it *was* dead.

As for its trunk, it was so thick it made the little blue saw look a toy. How could such a little thing destroy something so big. Sister Martha wondered if she would be able to join her hands round it. She would have liked to try, and to fail, just to make them all realize what Mother Audry was going to do. But already Mother Audry was fitting the saw's plug into Sister Agatha's socket. The saw gave a whirring shriek, and they all jumped. Sister Martha wondered whether Mother Audry had done that on purpose. Oh, if only she knew about saws and things, so when Mother Audry said, 'Can any of you explain . . .' she could say modestly, 'I think so, Mother,' and casually push the right button and feel Mother Audry watching her in a new admiring way. But of course there was no need. From another fold in her habit Mother Audry had produced an instruction leaflet – trust Mother Audry.

Mother Audry studied it for a long time. Past her arm, Sister Martha saw diagrams of bits of saw and pictures of trees caught in the act of falling. Presently Mother Audry returned the leaflet to her habit and rolled back her sleeves to the elbow. Sister Martha had never seen Mother Audry's arms before. They were strong and grey.

Suddenly Sister Martha knew what was going to be needed. To cut where the diagram showed, close to the ground, Mother Audry would have to kneel on the wet grass. Instantly she ran back down the side of the chapel, took a kneeling mat from the pile in the porch, came panting back and set it on the ground by the tree. For a terrible moment she wondered whether she had done wrong. Perhaps holy things from the chapel should never be used for other purposes, even when it was Christ's work they were doing. But strangely, Mother Audry neither blamed nor praised, but hardly seemed to notice.

'I shall cut here,' she said. She pointed to the base of the trunk, not where it was closest to the chapel wall, not sideways to the chapel, but in between.

'To allow a forty-five degree safety exit,' Mother Audry said. She pointed with her right arm down the chapel wall, then down the path where they were standing. She kept her right arm extended in this direction (like Christ turning out the money changers) for several seconds, before they understood and pushed each other quickly off the path.

Turning to the tree, she knelt, bent forward and set the saw's chain against the trunk. Again it whirred and shrieked. Sister Paula put her fingers to her ears to flatter Mother Audry by showing how much she was frightening her, but Mother Audry wasn't looking. She just held the shuddering, shrieking saw in her strong hands as its blade cut into the tree. Already the cut was as deep as the blade. If any of them noticed that the flying chips of wood looked fresh, they didn't mention it. After all, you couldn't expect a big tree like this to die all at once.

'Now I shall cut a notch on the other side,' Mother Audry said. To get there, instead of passing between the tree and the chapel, she stepped right across the path where it would fall. Sister Martha drew in her breath and bit the inside of her lower lip. A second later she was ducking forward to bring Mother Audry her kneeling mat.

'Keep back, child,' Mother Audry shouted at her.

Sister Martha stood still and shaking. Mother Audry was often stern, but never before had she seemed angry. Her anger was not impersonal, but for Sister Martha, and Sister Martha knew that it had been there a long time and only these anxious moments had let it escape. I was just trying to help, she wanted to say, but these words terrified her by their suggestion of criticism, and by the way she knew they would make her burst into tears. Instead she prayed, 'Please God make me more sensible.'

Mother Audry knelt on the path and began to saw at the underside of the tree. First she made a horizontal cut, then she made a cut angled down to meet it. Soon the piece in the middle began to joggle about as the saw still screamed. Then it fell out onto the path. It was like a big pale slice of cake. 'Well done', Sister Martha wanted to call.

Mother Audry returned to this side of the tree and to her first cut. It was so deep now that the saw was making quite a dull noise. Steam was coming out of the cut and there was a delicious smell of singeing wood. Mother Audry stopped the saw. Without turning, she said, 'I think someone is standing in the safety exit.'

It was true.

Soon the cut seemed to be more than half-way through the tree.

'Agatha and Martha, take the rope as far away as it will go,'

Mother Audry said, 'but don't pull till I tell you. Teresa, bring the wedge.'

Mother Audry set the wedge in the cut and gave it a kick with the underside of her shoe to fix it there. Again the wind came round the end of the chapel and this time surely it did move the tree. And down by the cut, it surely creaked.

'Now Paula, hit the wedge with your hammer.'

So it had all been arranged. Sister Paula was going to strike the blow which would bring down the tree.

From twenty yards away by the rhododendrons where she held the limp rope, Sister Martha watched Sister Paula striking the wedge. Her little stunted body swinging the long-handled hammer was like a dwarf's. Her blows on the wedge rang in the cold air, those which hit it and which weren't bosh shots on the trunk.

'I shall take a turn,' Mother Audry said.

At her first blow – a real blow – there was a much louder crack and the whole tree from trunk to topmost branches gave a quiver. Sister Martha was filled with an awful sorrow for it. It seemed wrong that they should be destroying something so big and old at so little cost to themselves.

'Right you are, Paula,' Mother Audry said, handing the hammer back to her. For the first time she gave a thin smile, as if even she was a little excited by what was going to happen, though more by Paula's excitement at the triumph she was about to have.

Sister Paula wound herself up for a bigger blow. She was bursting with pride, even from away by the rhododendrons Sister Martha could tell. She hit the wedge hard, but not cleanly. The head of the hammer must have been mostly beyond it because it whipped the handle out of her hand and the whole hammer spun away round the tree, finishing on the path at its far side.

But the blow had been enough. Now loud cracking and splitting sounds came one after another.

'Pull,' shouted Mother Audry.

Sister Agatha and Sister Martha pulled. At the same time Sister Martha looked up at the tree's upper branches, now swaying down towards them at terrifying speed. That was why she didn't see exactly what happened.

Afterwards it was all explained. Sister Paula, seeing the tree about to fall on the hammer which she had just used to knock it down, had made a dash to rescue it. Mother Audry had screamed at her and rushed after her, but tripped over Sister Agatha's cable and landed on her face. Perhaps the fall winded her because she had seemed to make no attempt to rise but had just lain there while the enormous tree gathered speed and came crashing down. Its trunk fell across her back.

'She's dead,' screamed Sister Teresa.

'Of course she's dead,' screamed Sister Agatha and was sick down the front of her habit.

'Oh oh oh,' screamed Sister Paula. 'It was me, it was me,' she screamed. 'Oh, oh, oh.'

Sister Martha ran to her where she stood staring down at the parts of Mother Audry they could see. Where her body emerged from below the great grey trunk horrible soft bulges seemed to fill her black habit.

'Come quickly,' Sister Martha said. She still couldn't touch Sister Paula. Then she did. She took Sister Paula's little red hand and made her run with her for help.

'It wasn't you,' she shouted as they ran. 'It wasn't anyone's fault.' But secretly she knew this wasn't true. It was she herself who had done it. God had known about her jealousy for Sister Paula and had said, 'All right, I'll show you where such wicked thoughts lead.'

The Return of the Moon Man

E. L. Malpass

This story was first published in *Esquire* – an American magazine famous for the short stories it publishes. The author is, in fact, Welsh and the story is set in rural Wales. It may be in the future but the Welsh folk in this story certainly haven't changed much. Mind you, the Electric is probably already at Pen-y-Craig. And there have been grandfather/grandmother jokes for a few thousand years.

A.D. 2500.

That was the year they brought the Electric to Pen-y-Craig Farm.

Wonderful it was, when Grandfather Griffiths pressed down the switch, and the great farm kitchen was flooded with light. There was Dai my father, and mother, blinking and grinning in the light, and Electric Plumber Williams, smug as you please, looking as though he had invented the Electric himself and sent it through the pipes. Only Gran was sad. Tears streaming down her face, she picked up the old paraffin lamp and carried it sadly into the scullery.

That was funny about Gran. She was progressive, and left to herself she would have filled the house with refrigerators and atomic cookers and washers. But Grandfather called these things devil's inventions, and would have none of them. And yet, when Grandfather at last agreed to the Electric, Gran was in tears. Reaction, Auntie Space-Ship-Repairs Jones said it was.

'Well,' roared Grandfather. 'There's your Electric. But don't think that because you've talked me into this you'll talk me into any more of these devil's inventions. Let no one mention the words space-ship in my presence ever again.'

That was intended for Gran. In her black clothes she was a rather pathetic-looking little woman, and no match for her fiery husband. But one thing she had always insisted that she wanted; a space-ship; and it had been a source of argument between them for years.

I tell you all this that you may know that we of Pen-y-Craig are not the backward savages that some people would have you believe. We are in touch with modern thought, even though we are apt to cling to the old ways. But what I really remember of those far-off, golden days of 2500 is of how the first Expedition to the Moon set off, and of how it landed in Ten Acre Field, and of the strange events that followed.

Men had been trying to set off for the Moon for years, perhaps for centuries. But you know how it is. Something always happened to stop them. The weather was bad, or someone's auntie died, or there was an eclipse. In the autumn of 2500, however, they were ready at last.

It was cold that evening, and we were sitting by the fire, enjoying the Electric. Grandfather was listening in; suddenly he jumps to his feet and shouts, 'Blasphemy.'

No one took much notice, for if the old man didn't jump up and shout 'Blasphemy' at least once of an evening Gran thought he was sickening and gave him a purge.

So Gran said dutifully, 'What is it, Mortimer?'

'Flying to the Moon, they are,' he cried. 'The space-ship has just left London. And they're dancing in the streets, and exploding fireworks in celebration. Sodom and –'

But at that moment there was a noise as of a great wind passing over, and then a terrible crash as though someone had picked up all our milk churns and dropped them on the Dutch barn. We ran outside, and there, in the Ten Acre Field, a Thing was glinting in the frosty moonlight. Huge it was, like a great shining rocket.

Grandfather looked at it. 'Lost their way, maybe,' he said with malicious satisfaction. Then he felt in his waistcoat pocket and took out a card and put it in my hand.

'Run you, Bronwen,' he said, 'and give them the business card of Uncle Space-Ship-Repairs Jones.'

But I was frightened, being but a little girl then, and clung to my mother's skirts. So Dai, my father, started up the tractor without a word, and rode off to fetch Uncle Space-Ship-Repairs Jones.

Down to the farm came the Moon Men, as the newspapers called them, their helmets bright in the moonlight, and soon Dai my father arrived. My uncle was sitting on the tractor with him, clutching a great spanner and grinning as pleased as Punch, and soon his banging and hammering came across the still air from Ten Acre.

One of the Moon Men took off his great helmet.

'Bit my tongue when we landed sudden,' he said.

'Nothing to what you will bite when you land on the Moon,' said my grandfather.

'That is what I am thinking,' the man replied. 'And that is why I say they can have their old Moon. Back to Golders Green by the first train it is for me.'

The leader took off his helmet at that. 'Go to the Moon one short?' he cried. 'That would never do.'

'I will go in his place,' said Dai my father quietly.

'You go? Never,' roared my grandfather. 'No son of mine shall go gallivanting round among the planets.'

My father flushed angrily. But no one argued with Grandfather, and at that moment we heard Uncle Space-Ship-Repairs Jones holloaing that the Moon-Ship was now as right as ninepence.

The Moon Men, all except the one who had bitten his tongue, set off for Ten Acre.

'I will come and see you off,' said Grandfather, and we watched him walk up the hill with the men.

With a great roar, the Moon-Ship rose into the sky, and climbed among the stars. Soon we could see it no more.

'Supper now,' said Gran.

We got the meal ready, and then someone said, 'Where is Grandfather?'

All the grown-ups looked uneasy, and suddenly I was frightened and began to cry.

'Gone to talk to the old bull, maybe,' said Gran.

Silently my father picked up the lantern and went out into the fields. It was a long time before he came back.

'Gone,' he said. 'Clean as a whistle.'

No one said anything.

Grandfather did not come back all night.

Nor the next day.

Then, at dusk, Read-All-About-It Evans, instead of dropping our evening papers from his helicopter as he flew past, landed. He marched into the house and thrust the paper under my father's nose, and said, 'See you.'

'Octogenarian on Moon,' said big headlines. Then, below: 'Radio flash from Moon party says Mortimer Griffiths, elderly Welsh farmer, took place of member of crew injured in earth landing.'

'Well, there is sly for you,' said my father. 'Going out for five minutes and finishing up on the Moon.'

Gran said nothing. But she went to the pegs and got her coat and went out of the door.

'Go with her, Bronwen,' my father ordered me, but kindly.

When I got outside it was almost dark, but a big, full Moon was just swinging clear of the hill, and I could see Gran going along the path that leads up Break Back and past Ten Acre and brings you to the Little Mountain. Though I was only a child I knew where Gran was going, and why. At the top of Little Mountain she would be nearer to the Moon than anywhere. I also felt, child though I was, that she would want to be alone, so I followed quietly, at a short distance.

Sure enough, Gran kept on up the mountain, and at last we were on the top place where there is nothing but broken rocks, and holes of black water, and lonely old ghosts. And the Moon was well up now, and so near that you felt that if you stood on tiptoe you could touch it like an apple on the tree.

Gran looked up at the Moon. And the Moon looked at Gran.

Now Grandfather was a big man, and I knew she was hoping to see him, perhaps putting up a little tent, or lighting a Primus. But there was no sign of anyone on the Moon's face. And at last, after a long time, Gran shivered and sighed. Then she muttered, 'Round at the back, maybe,' and she turned and came slowly down the mountain. And though she must have seen me she said no word.

The next night the same thing happened. At moonrise Gran set off for the mountain, and I followed. But this time the Moon was not quite round, and Gran looked at it for a long time. Then she said, 'Shrinking it is,' and came home again.

This happened every night. The Moon grew thinner and thinner, and Gran went out later and later. Young though I was, they let me stay up till all hours to follow Gran up the mountain. But at last the Moon rose so late that Dai my father said, 'Bed for you tonight, my girl.'

But I awoke in the small hours, and looked out, and there was the Moon, a thin, silver sickle, and there was the yellow light of a lantern climbing the dark side of the sleeping mountain.

I put on my coat and ran out into the cold.

When I reached the top of the mountain Gran was there. To my surprise she spoke to me. Pointing to the thin crescent she said, 'Hanging on by his finger-nails now he will be,' and she took my hand and led me home.

The next evening she said to my father, 'What time does the Moon rise tonight, Dai?'

My father looked at the paper.

'There is no Moon tonight, Gran,' he said.

'No Moon,' repeated Gran in a voice of death. 'No Moon.' She rose, and hung a black cloth over the big picture of Grandfather at the Eisteddfod.

'Falling through the sky he will be now,' she said slowly, as though speaking to herself. 'Like a shooting star he will fall, and like a shooting star he will cease to be.' She went back to her chair and sat down, her hands folded in her lap.

'But the fact that you can't see the Moon doesn't mean it isn't there,' my father explained. 'It's just that the sun is shining on the other side of it.'

Gran gave him a look. 'Black midnight,' she cried. 'Black midnight, and you talk to me of sunshine. Open the door.' She pointed an ancient finger at it. 'And, if the sun is shining, run up Snowdon barefoot I will, like the mad woman of Aberdaron.'

Dai my father gave up. There was a silence. Then Gran began talking again, almost to herself.

'He was a hard man,' she said. 'I didn't much care for him. Never would he buy me anything. A space-ship, only a little one, I asked him for, many times.'

' "No mention of space-ships in the Lives of the Great Saints," he says, smiling nasty, putting the tips of his fingers together, smug as you please.

' "No mention of indoor sanitation either," I say, real angry now. "But that do not stop Rev Williams having a little room up at the Manse."

'But it was no good. There was no arguing with Mortimer

Eisteddfod: a Welsh word. An *Eisteddfod* is a festival of poetry and music in Welsh

Griffiths.' She rose, and went to bed. And the next day she left for Aberystwyth and married Llewellyn Time Machine.

They went to 1954 for their honeymoon. And two days after they had gone Grandfather came back from the Moon.

'Finished the harvest?' he asked.

'Yes,' said my father.

'Have you mended the fence in Ten Acre?'

'Never mind the fence in Ten Acre,' said my father. 'Gran has married Llewellyn Time Machine.'

That was a terrible moment. For a long time my grandfather stood stroking his beard. Then suddenly he shot out his long arm and grasped a chopper.

'Where are they?' he roared. 'Where are they?'

My father, pale, said nothing.

Grandfather seized him by the throat and shook him.

'Where are they?' he repeated.

'In – in 1954,' gasped my father.

Grandfather let him go. 'Get the tractor out,' he ordered.

'Where are you going?'

'1954,' said Grandfather.

He was gone for nearly a week.

Then he came back, alone. He was in a good mood, quite talkative for him.

'Hired a Time Machine in Llandudno,' he said, beaming. 'Chased them right back to the Middle Ages. Llewellyn caught the Black Death. And I smashed his Time Machine to pieces with my little chopper.'

'And Gran?' asked my father.

'Stranded in the Middle Ages, with no money, and no means of getting back,' said Grandfather with immense satisfaction. 'She was taking the veil when I last saw her. Damp, the nunnery looked. Damp and cold.

'Teach her to go hankering after space-ships,' said my grandfather.

Trotsky's Other Son

Carol Singh

Carol Singh lives in Derby and is currently unemployed. She hopes that her writing (and she now has a number of published stories) will become very much her life. This story is set in the St Ann's district of Nottingham. The area has been completely rebuilt but was the city's worst slum. It was a maze of small bustling streets until quite recently. The old bookseller and 'revolutionary' is very much the central character and perhaps the 'I' is the author! As Carol Singh is suggesting, a label won't tell us much about the complex character of Michael.

Trotsky was the Russian revolutionary leader later driven into exile by Stalin and finally murdered. He was, under Stalin, made a bogey man to the Russians; there are still numbers of small would-be revolutionary groups who look to his ideas. And of course, quite a literature with a jargon of its own.

Some years ago I lived in that part of the city which was known as St Ann's. It was a sprawling area of industrial and pre-industrial houses set in cobbled hilly streets, to the north of the city centre. You walked along Parliament Street and turned down by the Milton's Head, passing the station and into a dirty old railway tunnel. Dim light from the constantly lit lamps shuddered around the tarred wooden walls and pools of rainwater in the mud floor. The smell of sulphur came strong and overhead was an arc of black nothingness shared with unseen rattling trains. The tunnel was dark and so long that when you walked down it you forgot about daylight and it always came as a shock at the other end.

Leaving the tunnel you stepped out blinking into St Ann's. Across the road, standing guard at the edge of the area like a grey fortress with its barred blank-faced windows, was a Victorian disease hospital, by this time devoted solely to treating venereal disease. Past the mass of the hospital the streets sloped down into Union Road, wide and dirty and noisy. House doors stood open, children and dogs and old people spilled from them on to the pavements. Pieces of privet and ancient lilac trees pushed their way up between slate roofs and outside lavatories. Willow herb lodged where it could. The pavements which were of many kinds of brick were stained with dust, spilt ice-cream, dog turds, rotting fruit, lolly sticks, bits of disintegrating cardigan and other matter which had irreparably lost its form and could only be guessed. Factories and churches and cream-painted pubs were pushed in between houses. In spite of the traffic packs of fat pigeons roamed about near the kerb edge and in the gutters, picking up spilt food outside the chip shops. They even crossed the road on their feet. Somewhere there was an ancient well dedicated to St Ann. Nobody seemed to know where it was. It had probably been built over in those days in the last century when, next to Calcutta, Nottingham had the worst slums in the British Empire. The oldest and dirtiest buses ran the circumference of the area. Teachers at the schools drove into St Ann's in the mornings and straight out again at four o'clock, leaving it untouched.

Turning by the Oliver Cromwell and into the main thoroughfare of Great Alfred Street, you saw a renaissance-style Methodist chapel, with pillars and portico and a wide sweep of steps, which was now a rubber-tubing factory. On the opposite corner was a secondhand bookshop. In its window an assortment of tatty paperback books was laid out in lines, and highly coloured American comics and packets of nylons and crayons were strung across the back of the window on a piece of string. A few dead flies lay scattered over the books, and a black cat was blissfully asleep in the sunshine which managed to penetrate through the dusty window. Here, like a yucca moth giving and taking from its plant, lived Michael Pat Jones.

Michael Pat was small, thickset and muscly, with large shovelly hands near his body, like a mole's, and he seemed to have a very large head, proportionate to his body as a baby's is to its body. He was nearly totally bald, and perhaps because of it his age was hard to place, he seemed old and yet unborn, there was something very foetal about him. He wore plastic tortoiseshell spectacles which had broken at the bridge, and he stuck them together by holding them over a gasflame until the plastic melted. As they kept on snapping and he kept on sticking them in this way he wore a progressively

the Oliver Cromwell: a public house or inn named after the seventeenth-century leader of the Parliamentary forces in the English Civil War

more owlish expression as his eyes seemed to get closer and closer together. From the front of the shop he sold secondhand books and comics, but in the back room he kept his duplicator ever turning, churning out documents and political statements and a weekly news-sheet. On the shelves around the walls were pamphlets, mostly by Lenin and Trotsky. The shop front was always pushing with children, and when he was working in the back room Michael operated a type of rigid prefect system worthy of the board schools. Any child caught thieving would expect – and get – very rough justice, St Ann's justice, from the boy in charge. There was great brutality in those days and in that place, and Michael was part of it. Hating still came completely naturally to him, he was not caught up with any ideas of social service or condescension.

Over the house was the smell of damp and cats. The stairs wound round twice, impinging into the rooms by the curves in its journey. The rooms were tiny, almost like large cupboards. There is something about tiny rooms which I like, they can be stultifying, smells linger in their brickwork, but you can expand your being and almost feel it hit against the walls, as though they are containing it, holding it whilst you grow. This can become intolerable, but it's better than wobbling disembodied in a vast room, or having all the objects in a well-planned room conspire against you. Michael Pat's room contained a low single bed heaped high with old blankets and about three old eiderdowns that different people had given him so he wouldn't be cold. Filthy curtains hung at the window, which was lodged permanently closed by a huge spanner which served instead of the catch, which was missing. The wallpaper in here, as in the rest of the place, was dusty and old and looked of the kind of pattern which fluttered from bombsites. Around three sides of the room were files and files of documents and old chewed newspapers and correspondence. The floor was littered with books and boxes of staples and rusting staples that had spilled from the boxes. Clumps of shoes were being attacked by mould. In a corner was a heap of dirty shirts which he periodically kicked aside in order to play on the lidless gramophone underneath his one record – 'Under Moscow Skies' – sung very slowly in French. The catch on the door didn't work, and so it was liable to bang all night if it was windy – the place

board schools: the schools working class children went to at the beginning of the nineteenth century, up to the age of eleven

was full of draughts and if the wind blew outside it blew inside too – keeping the occupants of the house awake.

I had left home to fly-stick and demonstrate during the Cuban missile crisis, and never went back. When you have spent several days thinking the world is about to be blown up things are never the same afterwards. There were many of us for whom that was true, and even many who did go home again afterwards were effectually driven from their families in spirit. Michael could be very stern. 'You must study.' And he pulled out a table from the heaps of mouldering documents and rubbish in his cellar, and set it up in my room for me to work on. 'The working class needs its people to know as much as they can. You owe it to your class as well as yourself to develop.'

For breakfast we all ate ice-cream from a van, even in the winter. Breakfasting from a tub of splintery ice with lashings of butterscotch was much better than being at boring old home eating boring old cereal before rushing off to boring old work. I was permanently afflicted with the adolescent curse of boredom. Michael boiled a kettle for tea practically non-stop throughout the day, and conducted fiendish sessions of mass egg boiling, enough to last several days at once, to save himself the bother of cooking. We ate pork chops with baked beans or lamb chops with peas – the lamb he casseroled in the oven by placing it in the frying-pan and balancing a rusty old cake tin over the top. I liked to watch him cook. It seemed as though it was just part of his function as a magician – a touch here, and there was a meal, a touch there, and there was an up-to-the-minute news-sheet and a room full of people waiting to staple it together and put it into envelopes.

He would suddenly take off for whole weeks with a moment's notice. 'Well I'm off now, if the bailiffs come round tell them the duplicator isn't mine . . .' The first time I heard this I was scared stiff, but I soon got used to it. His attitude to money was a mixture of disregard as to where it came from and indifference as to where it went. He took not the slightest notice of any bill until the final demand came. The gas bill would come. He would empty the gas-meter, find there wasn't enough money inside because he had paid the electricity bill with most of it, and so he would open up the coinbox on the telephone. Those bills and any connected with the

fly-stick: to stick posters on walls, trees, anywhere without permission

working of the duplicator were the only ones he paid fully. Other people were sent odd pounds whenever they complained. 'But that bill's for nine pounds!' I cried, the first time I saw him put a pound note in an envelope. He waved a hand dismissively, as though he was the creditor. 'Doesn't matter. This will keep them quiet.'

Michael Pat's first talk to us was on the relevance of Marxism to everyday life, and he used the simple example of the straw that broke the camel's back, to give us the idea of a qualitative change from a quantitative change. We were very young, and it was like being back at a kind of delightful school, with simple learning but no teachers. As Marxists, he said (with some exaggeration) we must recognize that everything, all matter, moved, always, that nothing stood still, and that attitudes based on the forcing of stasis or 'standards' or 'order' were both evil and – probably more important – futile. We must recognize that matter moved and changed and became transmuted, and learn to build upon that knowledge; never attempt to deny or thwart the movement or push of life. In a sense, he said, the parable of the shifting sands is incomplete: you had to build upon shifting sand because that was the only kind there is. Instead of being inauthentic adults whose only task in life was to carry out what our employers commanded, we suddenly became again children with invisible building bricks, getting the feel of impermanence, learning to create, destroy, create. My vocabulary book, abandoned when I left school, was pulled out of my old satchel and suddenly bursting with a crop of new words – helot, hegemony, latifundist, stakhanovite, putsch – words which thrilled me and that I wouldn't have learned then from any other source.

Michael's attitude to the children who came into the shop varied according to his mood. They regarded him with awe-touched suspicion, relieved by bursts of sudden completely unprovoked enthusiasm. He was authoritarian, but mad. He was liable to punch the boys and use extreme convoluted obscenities to them. He was merely extremely rude to the girls. This never made him unpopular. Many children whose parents were at work until five or six o'clock came straight to the bookshop from school, particularly in the winter, and Michael never turned them out even if they didn't buy anything. He told big lies about everything and everybody, and this seemed to appeal to the children. 'Here, are you really old Michael's stepmother?' I was asked by Alec, who helped in the shop. My mouth fell open, while the other children called and whistled and jostled by the paraffin heater. Michael often told them stories. One story which started its life in the back rooms had found its way, via Rocco, another of the boys who worked for Michael, into the shop. 'Be quiet, you lot,' he hollered, 'and when he comes back Michael'll tell you all about Trotsky's son.'

One of the pamphlets in the back room had been dedicated by Trotsky to his elder son – Leon Sedov, Son, Fighter, Friend – commemorated in epithets of granite. He had been murdered by Stalinists as he lay in a Paris hospital. This was very sad, but I was a nasty little thing and chockful of spite and I didn't like having my heart wrung. I preferred Trotsky's other son. I've never subsequently heard of him outside of the conversation of Michael Pat, and have no idea if he really existed. Michael claimed to have read a book about him, and so was constantly able to come out with nuggets of fresh information. When in what was our understanding Marxism became too much for me, I would insist, 'Tell us about Trotsky's *other* son.'

According to Michael Pat, Trotsky's other son wasn't political at all, the atmosphere in his home thick with politics since he was born merely bored him, and he ran off to join a circus. 'Let's see, what *was* his name . . .' He snapped his fingers trying to recall it. Michael told of the acrobats and the clowns, of Spangles the bareback rider who was in love with Trotsky's son ('Spangles?' mouthed the more sophisticated backroom contingent. 'Well you know what I mean. In translation,' was the impatient reply). But Trotsky's son didn't care about anybody except Mitsi, the pretty dappled horse who danced and curtseyed. He saved titbits for her, and when she led the other horses out into the ring his heart almost burst with excitement as she nodded her head to one of the clowns and danced in time to the music and people cheered. Michael told of his life from day to day, the hardships due to the famine and, as the revolution degenerated, to persecution by the authorities. Finally the circus was rounded up and sent to the salt mines, accused of misleading the masses. The conjurer was accused of 'deceiving the people'; the clowns of 'performing acts lacking in socialist content'. Then one time, whether due to a fit of pique or moral earnestness I don't know (probably the latter), Michael over-reached himself and etched in a deathbed conversion to Trotskyism in Siberia, and I never really believed in him after this.

Michael Pat escaped from St Ann's just before the sociologists descended, and treatises and theses were written, statistics compiled and analyses made of them. American photographers came with astronomically expensive cameras to photograph rats and rubbish. Shamed, the council made immediate plans to pull down the area, literally wipe it from the face of the earth. New concrete blocks have appeared, the old pattern of the streets and their Cromwellian names have been wiped out, and across the acres of rubble over Hutchinson Street many small fires crackle and smoke, like hellfire trying to break out. No longer walled up in his bookshop, Michael Pat moves around – London, Brussels, Addis, Paris . . . St Ann's is a long way behind him now. Most of us proved Michael's dismal expectations correct as to our revolutionary worthiness. We all reneged in one way or another, either from convenience or simple laziness. I haven't seen any of the comrades for years. But the other day on the bus I bumped into Alec, Michael's paper-boy. He is grown up now and married and working at Gedling Colliery. He asked if I'd heard anything of old Michael Pat. I shook my head. Then he turned and said with enthusiasm, 'Here, do you remember Trotsky's son and Spangles and the horse? I was telling my missis about that when we were courting. What happened to them in the end?'

The Wedding Jug

Philip Smith

This is another glimpse of family life seen through the eyes of an adolescent boy. It's more than that though. Grannie may be tiresome now and her daughter and grandson may have problems in living their own lives under her eye. But she had her day, and quite a surprising one!

Philip Smith is a member of a writers' group. He works part-time as a psychotherapist together with other odd jobs, and has been a teacher.

I stood at the back door and looked up at the moon. Its brightness from over the dark hump of the hillside made clear the pale drifting smoke from somebody's garden. The woodsmoke and the moon made me restless, eager to be moving in the sharp October night.

I had been standing on the door-step for several minutes, staring, wondering how on earth I was going to get through the evening. Saturday. Saturday night and I was stuck with my grandmother.

The others had gone – my mother and my sister, both courting. Neither of them seemed to care about my grandmother. Nothing much was ever said, they just went out, leaving her alone, or most often with me to sit at home because I just could not see that she should be left on her own on a Saturday night, with no one to talk to and everybody else out at the pictures or dancing.

Of course, *I* would have gone if I had been able to get away first. Then I would not have had to think about the old woman, plodding about the routines that she would fill her evening with. I would have slipped away and left my mother and Ena to argue, not with each other but with my grandmother, each separately conducting a running battle as they prepared for the night out. One of them would lose and the loser would stay at home, angry and frustrated at being in on a Saturday night, the one night of all the week for pleasure. Well, anticipation of pleasure. There was hardly ever any real fulfilment of hopes but at least the ritual of going out to the Queen's

Ballroom or the Plaza or the Regal brought with it a possibility and that was something to fight for.

'Where are *you* going?' my grandmother would demand of her daughter, forty-six and a widow for fifteen years.

'I'm going out.' My mother's reply would be even and she would look defiant as I imagine she had done at sixteen, and always would do.

'You're not going with that man are you?'

'What do you mean "that man"? You know who I'm going with and you know his name.'

'You should be ashamed of yourself, a woman of your age.' She was ready for a long session of baiting.

'I'm not a girl and I know what I'm doing. I deserve a bit of pleasure and I'm going to take it while I can. Damn it I've been at it all week skivvying, and you sit there like a queen, waiting for Annie to come in, and Annie to get your food, and Annie to do this and Annie to do that.'

'A queen? Sitting on my own in this house all night and nobody to say a word to? You don't care about anybody but yourself.'

And so it would go on until my mother would explode in a rage of swearing and tears and storm out through the front gate, running down to the corner of the street where Sid would be waiting.

Sometimes it would be my sister's preparations that my grandmother would notice first. Ena would be combing her hair and putting her lipstick on in front of the mirror over the living-room fireplace.

The old woman would have washed up the Saturday tea things and Ena would have wiped and they would have chatted quite happily as on any other weekday, but then she would be aware of the girl having slipped away while she was still emptying the bowl and wiping the draining board. She would notice Ena's quick, excited movements as she snapped her powder compact shut, and put it with her comb and lipstick into her handbag.

'You're not leaving me on my own are you?'

'It's all right, Gran, I'm only going to the pictures.'

'What time will you be back?'

'Oh I won't be long. I'll be back just after ten.'

'But what am *I* going to do? Here on my own.'

'Why don't you put the wireless on? And do some knitting. You'll be all right.'

'What – and me here on my own like some lost thing? I'm not staying here. I'm going. I don't know why I ever gave my home up, but I'll find somewhere. You'll see, I'll find somewhere. I'm not living like this any more. A dog wouldn't be treated like this.'

She would start taking her pinafore off – her sign to one and all that she was going to get her hat and coat.

At this point I would melt.

'It's all right, Gran. I'll be in. I'm not doing anything tonight. I'm going to be in.'

My sister would have slipped away. As far as I knew both she and my mother would spend their evening without a care. I was with the old woman, and if I were not, then she would still be all right. Nothing was going to happen to her. She'd be in bed when they got home and in the morning there would be Sunday dinner to prepare and that would make it easier to shut off from the complaining.

It was not like that for me, though. I just couldn't go if there was a chance that the old woman would be left alone. Sometimes my sister would decide to have a Saturday night at home if there'd been a tiff with a boyfriend or if her girlfriend had a cold, and I could go off with Ted and Ronnie and the others and feel contented. But, if there was any doubt, the thoughts of my grandmother would cloud my pleasure. In the middle of a film or on the bus home I would want to rush back quickly out of guilt and pity, anxious to find her happy and peaceful, hating the bickering that would last well into Sunday.

But tonight I had no worries about that at least. Whatever it was like, it would be a peaceful evening for both of us: for her, because she had me to talk to, and for me because my conscience would be clear and Sunday, at least, would be calm.

A double-decker bus, filled with people, and bright with yellow lights went by between the houses beyond the back gardens. A girl ran past the front gate, her high heels clopping on the pavement. She was followed by another, calling out to her to wait. A dog barked briefly and was answered by another in the distance. Then it became quiet. I turned on the door-step and went into the back-kitchen.

My grandmother was coming out of the living-room.

'I'll put some coal on and then we can have a nice fire.'

'It's OK, Gran. I'll get it.'

She took hold of my arm, her grasp tight and strong, and pushed me out of the way, gently.

'You sit down. Leave the fire to me.'

I knew there would be no winning of that argument. The rituals of building and replenishing fires were part of the rhythm of her life, and not to be disturbed. She would bend her arthritic legs painfully in the gloom of the coal-shed and swing the seven-pound hammer to break the lumps into just the sizes she needed.

I went into the living-room and got my book off the dresser. Thomas Hardy – *The Return of the Native*. I'd heard about Thomas Hardy at school: somebody had said he was as famous as Dickens, so that was good. I had trembled a bit in the library that afternoon when I had stood in front of the section where Hardy was. It was always like that starting a new author, thinking of all the things you never knew, things which were now going to be revealed to you.

I sat down in the 'basket-chair', a wicker chair that someone had given my mother because it had a few woodworm holes. On the other side of the fireplace was our other arm-chair, high-backed, with here and there a small split in the covering and a few horse hairs showing through.

My grandmother put the shovelful of coal down on to the fender and, with a slight grunt, picked up the iron poker and started to stir the fire. The fresh lumps were thrown on and she straightened up, the shovel hanging down by her side, in a faint haze of smoke and coal dust.

'Where's your pipe tonight?' she asked.

'It's over there.'

'Well, have a smoke. I like the smell. It shows there's a man in the house. I used to say that to Edward when he was alive.'

She went out through the back-kitchen to the coal-shed and I heard her throw the shovel down and turn the key in the lock. No more coal would be needed tonight. She shut the back-door and turned the key in the lock.

'Don't lock the door, Gran. Mam and Ena will be coming in.'

She gave no sign of having heard. She was washing her hands under the tap. It didn't matter: I could unlock it later. There was plenty of time.

The first small flames were beginning to come through the layer of small coal, lighting up the grey-brown smoke that was still thick in the chimney.

As I sat reading I was aware of her movements from the sounds: the bang of the cupboard-door under the sink as she got out the paraffin-can and a slight squeak as she unscrewed the top.

'Oh, that damn lamp! My head will never save my feet.'

I broke off from my book.

'I'll get it, Gran.'

'No, you stay where you are. You sit there. I'll go up and get it and then I can settle.' She put her hand on my shoulder, pressed me down, and grinned. I was aware of strength in her thin, white arm.

When Vivienne was with me I was glad of the times when my grandmother went upstairs to fetch her lamp. Sometimes on a Saturday we would both keep her company and would sit eagerly waiting for the chance to kiss whenever she left the room. As now, my grandmother would make her way slowly upstairs, and I would leap out of my chair to the girl, to kiss her, to squeeze her breasts, as much as possible before the old woman came back down. I could rely on my grandmother, though. There would be things to be done up there, even on a cold winter's night: the lamp-wick would need trimming, the lamp-glass would need to be breathed on and polished, something she needed for her knitting would have to be rummaged for in a drawer. And when she did come down, she would clump extra heavily on the lino of the stairs and give the loose doorknob a distinct rattle before she came back into the living-room.

She now walked to her drawer, took out her knitting and sat down opposite me.

I became absorbed by my reading, and a quietness settled in the room. The tapping of knitting needles and the occasional rustle of the now-glowing fire were sounds that touched only the outer edge of my mind. Occasionally I would look up as I turned a page, and note my grandmother in that repetitive and only half-conscious way in which a mother will check a sleeping child with a single there-and-back motion of the eyes. She was knitting a scarf, the only thing I had ever known her to knit, a long strip of red, brown, green, yellow, black in sections of random sizes according to the amount of wool she could find or unravel from some previous scarf that none of us could bring ourselves to wear.

I supposed that I would always connect my grandmother with knitting, and cream crackers, and pinafores.

In a little while, about eight-thirty, she would start to prepare her supper: cream-crackers and a cup of Oxo. These and porridge were the only things I had known her eat. 'Damn jockey's food,' she called it. She had long ago lost all her teeth and I could not imagine her with anything other than the sucked-in cheeks of a Mr Punch, and a wrap-round pinafore. We had only one photograph of her, taken in her forties, standing at her cottage gate, in her pinafore, with her sunken cheeks, smiling up at somebody, but old. She had never been other than old to me.

She bent forward now to pick up the poker and one of her needles clattered on to the steel fender.

'I'll do the fire, Gran.'

'No, no. It only needs a bit of a poke. You just pass me the tape-measure out of that jug.'

'Which jug?' I was looking at the shelves of the dresser. There were the Coronation mugs – mine and my sister's for George VI and Edward VIII, my mother's for George V, my grandmother's for Edward VII, and a miscellaneous collection of small vases and jugs and coloured glass dishes.

'That jug there by your hand. Yes, that's it. Give it to me; I'll find it.'

I handed her the glass jug, heavily patterned with embossed squares, and settled back into my chair. The wind seemed to be rising: the draught in the chimney was drawing the fire into a paler, hotter red. I rested both feet on the bars of the iron door of the oven next to the open fire.

'This was my wedding jug,' she said.

'Sorry. What did you say, Gran?'

'It was on the table on my wedding day. Full of rum.'

'Full of rum?' I had never tasted rum, nor even smelt it, but the thought of my grandmother being near a whole jug full of alcohol was deeply surprising.

'Yes, my mother had it filled with rum. We had it on the table in the village hall, in a big white, starched table-cloth. Edward and I – Edward, that was your grandfather – sat at the top end of the table. It was lovely. We had a jug of rum and a jug of sherry and a jug of whisky and a jug of port wine.'

'Did you drink all that?'

'Course we did! It was a hot day. We had a table full of things and a lovely white cloth that my mother had. We had boiled ham and pickled onions and tomatoes and plates of bread and butter, and currant bread and currant cake.'

'Did you have a wedding cake, Gran?'

She seemed not to hear this.

'Do you know – in the middle of all that I saw a little boy standing at the door of the hall. He stood there with his cap in his hand, looking, and then he saw me and came up to where I was sitting. He had been running and he was sweating. I always remember that – he had little drops of sweat across here (she ran a forefinger along her upper lip). He was holding something in his right hand. It was a clean, white handkerchief, folded. He said, "I've brought a present for you," and he gave me the handkerchief. It had something wrapped in it. I took it in my hand like that (she opened her left hand, palm uppermost, and made delicate gestures of unfolding with the thumb and forefinger of her right hand) and I opened it. Do you know what was in it? A gold watch. Very thin. A very, very thin gold watch. Very delicate. I knew whose it was. It was Tommy's. He was very proud of it. It had belonged to his father – and he'd sent it to me on my wedding day.'

'Who was Tommy?'

'Tommy? He was my lover.'

I had been staring into the fire, grasping every word with my head down. Now I looked up and met my grandmother's eyes. They were calm and, I noticed for the first time, bright blue in the withered skin.

'You see, I had two of them – him and Edward. I had to choose, didn't I? I couldn't go on with the two of them. It had to be the one or the other. I couldn't go on messing about with two.'

I nodded as though I knew, but my stomach trembled at the thought of a woman 'messing about'. My chest was pounding at the picture of a woman with two men – and two men with one woman.

'He was such a tender boy – Tommy – so gentle . . .'

She smiled, as though recalling a child.

'– but – I married your grandfather.'

I tried to make my voice casual with the question.

'Why did you choose Edward, Gran?'

'Who knows?'

I noticed that she had breathed in deeply, and was almost sighing as the breath came out. There was suddenly a tiredness about her. 'Who knows?' she said again.

'Anyway – on the day of my wedding Tommy sent me a present. He sent me his lovely, thin watch. And then – do you know what he did?'

I could feel my head lowering, and had to lift my chin and raise my eyes to meet hers. She held my look, as though I were leaving for a long journey.

Her voice was even and clear. She said:

'He went out into his mother's garden – to the big apple tree there and then he hanged himself.'

The old woman sat upright, looking now into the darkening glow of the fire, the glass jug cradled in her hands on her lap.

There was a rustle as the embers settled on to the bottom of the grate and one or two flecks of ash were carried by the smoke up into the chimney.

The Man

Jane Stone

Children feature a lot in short stories. Perhaps it is because they live so much in the present, event by event. A child's life is, in a way, a sequence of short stories. But through the child's eye, we can often see things about the way grown-ups feel and behave in a way we could not do for ourselves. And we also have the pleasure, if that is the right word, of finding our experience of the world giving an adult meaning to what the child so innocently records. It is a double or treble take, of course; after all, the author is adult!

This story by Jane Stone starts like many children's adventures. There is a mysterious house and a strange inhabitant. But it doesn't turn out like the books – except that the children learn something the adults do not know.

No one knew when he came to the village. All that the adults, those proud possessors of worldly knowledge, could tell us was, 'He came.' One night, it was late September, and the house stood empty, as it always had, and we went up scrumping apples as we always had – well, no one claimed them now. The leaves were wet and soggy underfoot, and we frightened ourselves with tales of ghosts evolving out of the thin spirals of mist which wrapped around the trees.

That was the last time we ever climbed the apple tree, or watched the squirrels scurrying through the leaves to bed. The last time, that is, in play. The next night, the gate was locked, fences repaired, and lighted windows fended off even Johnny McCrae, who lost much status in consequence. But by far the most important thing was the old man who stood peering out of the curtainless windows downstairs. He wasn't very tall – he was stocky – he had a bushy moustache, thinning hair and he wore 'sort of baggy pants,' said Andy.

scrumping: a term used, usually by children, to describe the taking of apples or other fruit from trees in other people's gardens or orchards

'Like a clown,' described Mary-Lou, but 'plus fours', corrected the grown-ups. 'Country gentleman's wear,' they added reverently – but we thought it a stupid name, for 'Plus means add,' said Andy. 'And four what?' he said.

For days after that we asked ourselves, 'Who is he?', bitterly resenting the interloper who had taken over our playground at such short notice. Until, one day, 'We gotta find out,' stated Andy. And when Andy stated anything, we did it.

That night the seven of us met, scared stiff, at the gates of the house. It was late now, and a solitary light flickered above the door. It came from the only room with curtains – at least at the front of the house. It was dark, and silent, and 'Let's go back, then,' whimpered Angie McClean, who always was a coward and never improved. 'Let's go *on*!' we said, in chorus.

Up the silent path, my heart jerking the strings of my cotton pinafore; up the path and across the strip of lawn we went. No one spoke because no one wanted to. That is a way with children. The stillness pressed upon us from behind, driving us up, up, into the relative sanctity of the long dark windows. Andy, longing to show off his knowledge of house-breaking, was as eager as a young bloodhound. It was common knowledge that Andy's brother had been the best clickie in the West Riding and it was also common knowledge that Andy showed promise far beyond his years. But as it happened that promise wasn't to be displayed. The door was open.

Andy's brother had not outrun his uses, however. From his pocket Andy produced a huge torch, with a beam so powerful that it illuminated the whole of the room we entered. It was a lovely room, long and high and spacious but, 'Heck!' said a disappointed Andy, 'It's empty.' And so it was. No carpets, no chairs; no heavy ugly dressers, concave mirrors, plaster dogs and plastic flowers such as made up the comfortable familiarity of our own homes. More sad than all these; the room was clean. Gleamingly, spotlessly clean. Our spirits fell, but, 'We might as well go on,' said Jo – so we crossed the room.

The door didn't creak as we opened it, like doors in mystery stories or the *Ghostly Tales* book I'd just been reading. No, this door was smooth, varnished, well-oiled. The hall into which it led was, surprisingly, circular, with a floor patterned in tiles of ivory and

clickie: a slang term. A clickie is good at picking locks

gold. In the centre stood a type of plinth – 'for a statue,' whispered Jo – but the statue must have gone visiting, and the hall was clean and bare.

We crossed the hall, forgetting for an instant to be silent, pulling up short, poised, ready to fly, as our serviceable steel-tipped shoes made contact with the tiles. 'Hope this'n's locked,' said Andy, darting towards the door. 'Wunna be,' stated Johnny. 'There inna nothin' worth takin'.'

He was right. It wasn't locked. And neither were any of the other doors. And not a single stick of furniture, thread of carpet or speck of dust did we see in any of them. The kitchen was of most interest, with a sink and a stove but, 'No food,' I said, in disappointment. I always was the greedy one.

So there we stood, a depressed little group, bunched at the foot of the stairs, debating whether to go on or back. Andy had just set his foot upon the bottom stair and Jo had turned towards the door when Angie McClean was sick. We looked at her in horror and we turned and ran.

Yet the next day, our appetite for the mystery was keener than ever. We organized a watching day to observe the movements which could be seen so clearly through the uncovered windows. There were six of us, so we split into twos and took shifts; Johnny and Mary-Lou for the morning, Andy and Jo for the afternoon, and Jimmy and me for the evening. Angie McClean, since her lapse of the previous day, was banned from our company.

By the end of the day we knew most of the man's movements. He rose late in the morning – by our standards at least, for we were mainly farmworkers' children and used to being up with the milk. Johnny and Mary-Lou, crouching in the orchard, watched a front window flung wide open, and there he was, short, stocky, 'in black pyjamas!' stated Johnny importantly, 'Black pyjamas, an' then he –' 'What?' we shouted in exasperation. 'He sorta jumped an' waved his arms about an' then' – his voice dropped to a whisper – 'he takes his clothes off, an' jumps about with nothin' on!' 'He does *not* then,' broke in Mary-Lou sharply, 'You can never tell anythin' straight Johnny McCrae. He had his trousers on.'

Then the man disappeared for a while, presumably for food, though where he had it we did not know. It occurred to us, though, that the upstairs rooms might possibly be more homely than those downstairs. Mary-Lou and Johnny had filled in the time by exploring the outhouses and found: 'Wood,' said Johnny, 'little tiny bits of wood, all done up in bundles.' 'And cloth,' broke in Mary-Lou excitedly, 'little packs of silk and stuff – all laid out on a table.' We wondered if he could be a carpenter, or a tailor, but 'there wasn't enough of anything,' said Johnny, 'Not to make things.'

After the exploration, they had picked up a few large apples, and sat in the shrubbery, munching and waiting. Some time later, the man came out through the front door and took a turn round the grounds. He walked carelessly over the damp garden, his heavy boots plodding aimlessly over rotting apples, brilliant michaelmas daisies and fallen rotten leaves. He stood for a while peering up at the gnarled apple trees, loaded with fruit. Then he went inside and reappeared, armed with a curved stick, and attacked the branches with it. Hearing this hurt us most of all, for we had become so used to regarding the apples as our own particular property; it hurt us to think of their beautiful ripe redness as they tumbled higgledy-piggledy upon the grass. It hurt us to hear how the old man had gathered them up in a huge basket, taking them who knew where; perhaps to that high-up room of his. The damsons, too, were picked – 'the pig,' Mary-Lou had said, her mouth open and watering; 'he can't possibly want them all.'

He had come out on to the terrace afterwards, with a pipe and a glass of beer, and sat, legs stretched out in front of him, alternately sipping and puffing, squinting at the tossing trees through the smoke. Then he disappeared again. Johnny and Mary-Lou watched and waited, as minute after minute went by, to try to get some inkling of what was going on. At length, they grew quite bold, leaving their hiding place in the shrubbery and going right round the house to see if they could see into the upstairs rooms. But there was no sign of movement, and when Andy and Jo came to relieve them, they shook their heads in disappointment.

Andy and Jo hid themselves in the orchard for the afternoon watch. 'He has his food upstairs, out of tins,' said Andy; and this wasn't all guesswork, for he was a good sleuth, and had spent some time educating himself with the contents of the dustbin, 'Sardines, baked beans, and – Spagg Hetty,' said Andy. None of us had heard of spaghetti before.

'And after his food?' we asked – if it *was* after his food – 'but I think it must be,' said Jo, 'because he sleeps.' 'Outside,' put in Andy; 'Even though it clouded over he still sat outside.'

Then came the operation that we knew must happen sometime – the time we'd been waiting for. 'A man, dusting and polishing,' scowled Andy, in disgust. 'An' why not?' said Jo. 'He's not got a woman.' 'But me *Dad* wouldna do it,' said Andy, as if that set the seal on things.

Jimmy and I came on duty just after tea. Ours was the dullest time of the day. We watched the light come on in the mysterious upstairs room, the only room with curtains. And all we could see were shadows. Shadows flickering here and there over the blinds; now a hand, now an arm, now some strange stump-like object waved about like a witch's wand. Crouching there in the damp leaves, with the mist just beginning to rise, we felt ourselves hard done by. 'Nothing happenin',' grumbled Jimmy. 'We gotta explore them rooms.' 'But not alone,' I said. I did not want him to think me a coward so, 'it wouldn't be fair to the others,' I said. Jimmy gave in, and we spent the rest of the evening munching sweets and windfalls, huddling together for warmth in the clammy mist, speculating about the strange ritual in the upstairs room. 'He probably murders rich women,' fancied Jimmy, 'cuts their clothes up and makes them into new cloth and then dries their bones to make wood.' I imagined my own bones joining that little pile of sticks and felt sick. 'I must know,' I said. 'Right,' said Jimmy, 'tomorrow night!'

By the next night we were tired of uncertainty, and walked boldly up to the windows, and into the room; we wasted no time there and went straight through the hall, though I noticed as we entered it that it was now clean and shining again.

We climbed the curved wooden staircase and found ourselves on a narrow landing with five doors opening off it; two one side, two the other, and one straight ahead – 'The Room,' whispered Andy. We stood for a moment and heard the sound of heavy breathing from a far door. 'He's in there,' said Jo: 'Come on.'

Silently we approached the end door. The door swung open, and Andy's torch flung the room into daylight.

We were spellbound. We even forgot to close the door in our awe. For the room was lined with deep, broad shelves, about eight to every wall. And from each shelf, regarding us unblinkingly, almost insolently, rows and rows of '*dolls*?' said Andy, hesitantly, and his hesitation was not surprising, because 'They look ALIVE,' we breathed. Blue eyes, black eyes, brown eyes, smiling, staring, frowning, sulky, incurious, shining, sad, eyes flashing at us from faces that looked as if they should be soft and warm but, 'they *are* dolls,' said Johnny, as he poked one with his finger-tip.

There were sailor dolls, soldier dolls, beautiful girl dolls, bride dolls, fairy dolls, and best of all, foreign dolls. Dolls from almost every country in the world: sultry velvet-eyed maidens from the East, dark-haired vivacious señoritas from Spain, and prim little Dutch girls in clogs. I longed to cuddle the little fat Eskimo who smiled at me, it seemed, with fellow feeling. All were so exquisitely dressed that I couldn't see how anyone, least of all a man, could do such work.

'D'you think they move?' asked Josie at length, after our eyes had explored the long room. She stretched out her hand and took up a ballerina doll. It was fixed to a round wooden base, and behind it there was a key; Jo grabbed it and began to turn.

The ballerina doll had been poised on both toes, her arms reaching up above her head. Now, as Jo turned the key, the arms began to move, a little jerkily, swaying gently to a tiny, silvery tune, 'Like a musical box,' Andy told us. 'It's the music from Swan Lake,' breathed Mary-Lou, who went to weekly ballet class.

So enthralled were we by this spectacle that we forgot the open door. We forgot that we were in someone else's house, with that someone sleeping only one door away. We forgot to whisper, and forgot our steel-tipped shoes. And so we were terrified by the roar which suddenly came from behind us.

We turned, cowering, and met the man face to face. He was smaller than we thought, and stockier. His eyes were small, too, and now they glittered, deep blue and cold and clear, like blue sky over snow. His black pyjamas were no longer a cause for laughter – now they seemed horrific. We stood – he stood – and between us the little ballerina dropped to one knee as the last silvery strains of her music faded away.

He stood there, and his face was set in hate. He almost spoke, and then seemed to change his mind. He turned and strode out, slamming the door behind him. We half expected a key to turn, but it did not.

Yet we made no move to escape. By some kind of tacit general consent we all sat down on the floor. 'If it'd been me Dad,' said Jimmy uneasily, 'he'd have walloped us.' We nodded, for the thought was in all our minds. It bewildered us to be left thus, with no retribution: not even a long cussing which, by experience, we had all grown to expect from irate adults.

'He'll be waitin' for us downstairs,' said Johnny. But somehow we felt he wouldn't, and we felt guilty and uneasy. 'But we haven't *done* anything,' persisted Mary-Lou, 'only looked.' 'That's not it,' I said; 'they wasn't ours to see.'

'C'mon,' said Jimmy, standing up, 'we gotta say sorry.'

I shouldn't think any of us had ever said sorry to a grown-up in our lives – at least, not in a voluntary way. It just wasn't done. You had your walloping, and you moped for a while, and then everything went on as usual. Or else in really serious matters you were locked in your room until hunger forced an embarrassed kind of apology. But this was different. We stood up in a body and went to seek the man.

He was in his room we knew, for we could hear him moving about. Jimmy knocked on the door. After a while it opened a little and, 'I thought you'd've gone,' said the voice – surprisingly mild.

'We came to say . . .' Jimmy's voice trailed off. It was more difficult than he expected. 'Sorry,' almost shouted Mary-Lou, helping him out. 'Sir,' she added, remembering her manners.

The door jerked open suddenly: and he was smiling! He was smiling all over, and the black pyjamas were eclipsed by a bright red dressing gown. 'Well,' he said; 'that's the most difficult part of all. Come in.'

It was one of the oddest, yet pleasantest hours of my life. We were right about his food, because he produced a huge loaf from a cupboard filled with tins and he lit a gas ring in the corner of the room. We made huge piles of hot toast and loaded it with butter; and we made cocoa with evaporated milk that tasted like cream. For a while we were all too busy eating to talk, and his appetite, we noticed with satisfaction, was as keen as ours; we were too well used to the delicacy of grown-ups, who stopped after two sandwiches or one piece of cake and made you feel a pig if you asked for more.

So it wasn't until we slowed down a bit and started on chocolate biscuits and a large slab cake, that he asked us, 'What made you come?'

We looked at each other, and then Jimmy began to speak. He usually did the talking. He told him everything; about the garden, the apples, the watching, and the room. He told him how we had loved the dolls, and at the end he asked, 'Why d'you keep 'em all locked up, sir? Why don't you let people see 'em?' The old man extracted a large cherry from his piece of cake. 'It's a long story,' he said. 'And I'm not going to bore you with it.' I opened my mouth to say we wouldn't be – but closed it again on a warning look from Andy.

'Once,' said the man, 'I was married. Like most people. And like most people, I was happy. My wife was never strong, and three weeks before she had our baby she was ill. She died when our daughter was born.'

He spoke sadly, but without embarrassment, and so we felt no embarrassment either. This was odd, because in our homes, if anyone discussed birth, it was in a hushed voice, and with lowered eyes, which made us feel hot all over, and sometimes we were sent right out of the room.

'But you had your little girl?' I said – and then wished I hadn't, the man looked so sad.

'I had my little girl,' he said. 'But she couldn't walk or talk. She sat. Just sat.'

We said nothing.

'But don't think I didn't love her,' he said forcefully. 'She was my wife all over again. I made her dolls. She watched me while I made them, and I knew she knew I loved her and was making them for her – and I knew she loved them, so I made more and more. And when she died,' we sat unblinking, for we had been prepared for this; 'And when she died, before she died, she stretched out for her dolls, and over the dolls her eyes looked at me – so gratefully. I swore I'd go on making them. But they're *hers*, you see. No one else must see them. They're for her.'

'And then we came and saw them.' It was Jimmy again.

'Ah, well.' The old man stood up and he suddenly looked tired, 'You're children, after all. And what are dolls for, if not for children? I did not make them for myself. They were for her.'

Quietly he opened the door.

It was a signal for us to go; and we obeyed it. We shuffled out, and, turning, Jimmy had the last word.

'I'm sorry we upset you, sir – but I'm glad we come.'

We never went there again. Sometimes we thought of the lovely overgrown garden – the jungle-like shrubberies, the broken branches we collected for Guy Fawkes' night, the climbable gnarled old trees – and as the blossom lent its fragile whiteness to the apple orchard we thought with regret of those rich red apples that autumn would bring. Sometimes, in the clear, sweet mornings of spring, we would think of the dolls, shut away in their curtained room: blank little eyes that never saw the sunlight, or the garden, or the springtime flowering of the shrubberies. And sometimes, we thought of the old man himself, and even thought he might like to see us again; but we hadn't been asked, and (with the quicksilver minds of children) we always had something else to do. In fact, now we knew the secret, we scarcely dwelt upon it; we were too practical to weave fantasies about it, too sensible to invite the scepticism and ridicule of the whole child population of the neighbourhood by telling our friends a story which they, and we, too, if it had been told to us, would have met with cries of 'The old cissy!' or 'Don't be so wet', or 'Give over, will yer, can't yer see I'm crying?'

So we dismissed the house, the man, the grounds, and life went on much as before. The long hazy summer days deepened again to autumn, and the corn began to be gathered from round about. The apples began to form upon the trees; acorns and bright polished conkers littered the ground. We collected blackberries glowing in the hedgerows, and wild hips and haws.

And then we noticed something strange about the old house. It was Johnny who first put it into words. 'Them apples is coming down,' he said. It was so, and the brilliant redness grew and grew upon the ground and still they were not gathered. The harsh bitter-sweet smell of rotting fruit began to grow, and now and then another would drop to its fellows with a splash. 'D'you think he's O.K.?' inquired Johnny at length.

We bore it uneasily for a few more weeks, but it was when the damsons began to fall that I said to Jimmy, 'We'll have to tell someone.' So, unwillingly, we told my mother, who shook her head and told us to run away and play.

It was two days later they buried him, and no one went to his funeral. We knew, because we tried to go, but the vicar and the sexton chased us off without listening to our explanations. Later, I heard my mother talking. 'Yes,' she said, 'they found him dead in bed. Awful old man – don't know what he did with himself. Some kind of hermit, most like – no, nothing in the house. All empty. So they just took him and came away.'

'And no one knows who he was?' queried my father.

'No. No family at all, s'far as they can make out. No job – like I said – it's not as if he *did* anything.' To my parents, this was the deadliest sin of all.

I turned away. I longed to burst in and tell her – 'you're stupid, you are, you're blind! Didn't you look in the little room – the one with a lock? Didn't you *see* them? The dolls, the dolls – the beautiful dolls?'

And then I remembered him saying, 'They were *hers*, you see. They were *hers*.' And I imagined what might happen to those dolls and I felt they might be better after all, up there, alone. And most of all, I knew what my mother would say if I tried to tell her what we saw.

So I picked up my coat and ran out into the autumn rain. And who knew that it wasn't the rain that damped my cheeks.

Nothing Has Changed

Colin Thubron

Colin Thubron started his career in documentary film and in TV. He made his reputation, though, as a travel writer, especially in the Middle East. He has more recently turned to novels. There is a journey in this story; it is an exploration of the writer's own feelings when faced with both his loss and someone else's. Whether the woman in the story really existed or not does not matter; the situation is a very human one.

We writers seem condemned to scratch the ground for buried unhappinesses, like pigs snuffling after truffles. Whether from catharsis or masochism – suffering is our stock-in-trade. Love affairs, bereavements, sickness – we pass through them all with, it is said, an embarrassing excess of sensitivity. Then we utilize (and betray) everything that has happened to us. We do business with our neuroses. We even grow rather fond of them, in a proprietorial way. They become our distinction.

So I give you this woman, lying in a hospital bed in Reading (I'm sorry, but even neuroses come in clichés). Her face was always pale, so it's hard to see if, in this clinical light, she is whiter than in ordinary life. The room around her is white too, and the sky in the window. Even the ruffled sheet and the pillows are mounded about her like a recent snowdrift.

When I take her hand she lets out a faint, irritated moan and suddenly shivers in the bed, pushing her feet down like a dancer trying to lift herself on point. Even after fourteen years she looks unchanged. The girl in my memory is merely a little plumper and her boyish coronet of hair has now flowered into an exotic auburn tangle which spreads blackly over the pillow. As I remember, it is the face's bones which are important and strange: they look evanescently fragile, as if they have lent their own whiteness to the flesh that barely covers them.

point: ballet term – on the tips of her toes

She is – indefinably – beautiful; and the expression on her face, as her eyes open and before she has recognized me, holds the familiar look of unprotectedness, impossible to locate in any particular feature.

She whispers: 'Oh Christ.'

'I'm sorry. Is it a shock?'

A faint smile. 'How the hell did you know?'

'By chance. Your parents. They said you were back in England. Operation and convalescence, they said.'

She didn't answer. She lifted her hand tiredly from mine, then let it fall. Its inert warmth dropped against my fingers. Her gaze was flickering over my face (what was she seeing? Receding hair, some wrinkles) but avoided my eyes. The room was filling up with questions. I didn't know which ones to ask. None of them were my business, and she refused to make things easier by saying anything, but simply lay faintly smiling and not looking at me, even though our fingers were now entwined.

In the end I said: 'Is he still in Hong Kong then . . . your husband?' I couldn't call him Robert.

'Yes. He wasn't able to get away.'

He wouldn't, I thought. Instead he'd paid for a private room in a top hospital. When I glanced round, the only sign of affection I saw was a vase of tulips wilting on a window-ledge beside a Get Well card from her mother. But then she probably had few friends left in England, after so long.

I pressed her hand against my face, from pity or simply habit, I don't know. How did she expect me to behave? I had only ever known one way of being with her, and it seemed too late to evolve another.

She was staring at me. 'You haven't changed.'

I passed a hand across my face.

She added: 'You haven't married.'

'No.' My stomach seemed to be emptying. 'I don't think you've changed either.'

She gave an odd laugh. She was looking at the shape of her thin body under the sheet, touching her palms over her stomach. She said very quietly: 'I have now.'

'But the operation was successful.'

'Yes.'

Whether it was her pallor (a little frightening now) or her habitual look of vulnerability or simply the angular fragility of her body under the nightdress I don't know, but I felt a foolish rush of tenderness for her. I half stood up, and clasped the softness of her shoulders in my hands. 'They told me it wasn't cancer.'

'No. Endometriosis.'

I knew, of course. I'd looked it up. And I supposed it was that growth (the medical books made it sound like black-spot) that had prevented her conceiving children in the first place. 'Did they have to remove . . . everything?'

In the silence the question grew huge, impertinent. I had not seen her for fourteen years. A married woman. Her shoulders were trembling in my hands. She looked up at me and said: 'Most of it. I can't have children, if that's what you mean.'

Yes, my love, that is what I meant. Not only your children, but mine (because after all these years I still love you, I couldn't marry anyone else). You think my grimace of sorrow is only for you, of course, but it's for me too, and for our unborn, our never-to-be-born sons and daughters. Your whole body is shaking in my hands. Suddenly, realizing, you twist your head and kiss my fingers. You say: 'I always wanted your children.' I see my tears falling on to the sheet.

Evening. Driving back to London, I pass her old house. I must have done this once a month for fourteen years (whenever I return from seeing my parents) and have scarcely given it a glance. Her family left it years ago, and in any case the yellow-brick façade, with its Victorian windows, is like a theatre set. Its memories lie unseen behind: in the passages, the sitting room, the enclosed garden.

I stop and ring the doorbell. Whoever opens the door will seem an impostor, of course, a caretaker. I ring the bell again. It makes the same noise as fourteen years ago: a dry shrillness in the bowels of the house. I know now that nobody will come, and that seems right. Nobody to replace the nineteen-year-old girl, who used to throw open the door so quickly that it might have been done by someone invisible. And always the surprised 'It *is* you!' as if she had expected somebody else, or been afraid I wouldn't come.

I walk round to try the garden gate. It opens. In the fragrant enclosure nothing has changed. Two flagstoned steps descend from the French windows into a tangle of spring-flowering shrubs. The neighbours' wall at the end shows the same patina of grey-blue lichen. The whole garden is barely thirty foot deep, and narrow. Behind my back the house windows hang dark. I close the garden door softly behind and stare down the shrub-avenue. For some reason I'm frightened. Close to where I entered, everything is all right. She is watering plants in a summer dress (it's always summer), swinging the can back and forth in her long, impatient fingers. But a few paces beyond, just out of sight of the house windows, a grass clearing laps against the patinated wall. I remember it perfectly, although I can't see it yet. I pause among the sheltering shrubs. I feel cold and slightly sick.

Because there, by the wall, in the clearing (which I haven't entered yet), her back is turned. She is tense, angular, nineteen. She wears an old check coat and jeans. She won't look at me. Her hands are thrust into her pockets and she stands perfectly still as if she were gazing across fields.

I say: 'It's Robert, isn't it?'

She half turns round, but keeps her eyes averted. The slope of one cheekbone shows white and hard. She says: 'I'm going away.'

Then I hear my voice as if it were someone else's: it's oddly vibrant. I'm twenty years old: tender and resolute. 'I'll be here when you get back.' I'm conscious of standing under the copper beech, the tallest tree in the garden, the only real tree. It's spread above me like my own strength. I half raise my arms, to partake of it. I see myself in her eyes, under the copper beech: its trunk, my body. 'You know I love you.' She's looking at me now. 'Always.' I was young, of course, too young to know about Always (but I was right just the same).

She said: 'You can't.'

I want to reach out to her, but the distance is enormous, and suddenly she looks foreign, neuter even, and I'm still saying 'I love you' when she walks away.

This part of the garden was always different from the rest. It is dominated by the lichened wall. I stare back at the house to make sure I'm not seen. I'm a trespasser here now, in my past. I walk backwards for a few seconds looking up at the empty windows, and then turn into the clearing. It is so very simple. There is nothing that could have changed: just brick and grass.

But there is no tree.

There is no room for any tree, let alone a full-grown copper beech. I stare at emptiness. I am not exactly surprised. But I feel a heavy distant shock, as if something had fallen in another room. I search the grass for a bole, but I know already that there won't be one. There has never been one.

That's the trouble with us writers. We write these fictions into our lives for our protection. (The imaginative person, after all, can believe anything.) But only now am I shocked by the gathering of the memory, the lie. All these years. In place of the beech there is only a circle of cold sky. This is unaltered.

So I will try to find the truth again before it goes. As I stand here, the facts of the place – wall, grass – encase even me (the slippery writer) in a frame of honesty. What is really remembered? Something young and desolately commonplace.

Fear. We are moving too fast to the finality of marriage, and I can't (I am still living in an adolescent world of infinite possibility: I will live for ever). I talk about a trial separation. I am too self-accusing to be gentle. My words rasp and stumble in the clearing, while her upturned face flinches and I watch her close herself off. Her eyes, and then her whole body, slowly turn themselves away, and suddenly her narrow back in the check coat is formidable with its wound, and the five feet between us are immeasurable. My voice is a bleat. 'You know I love you.' (Trying to save dignity.)

She says: 'I'll go away.'

I'm leaning against the wall like a rag doll. 'Robert . . .'

But this makes her angry. She doesn't turn round but shouts into the shrubs. 'You know I don't care for him! Don't make him your excuse!'

I repeat feebly, without belief: 'I do love you.'

But she says 'You can't', and when she turns, her face is irreparably changed. Her voice too: it contains a kind of premonition. It is as if she had known everything before. 'This is all fantasy to you, isn't it? It's not real. It's just words and attitudes. Just romanticism. You don't really feel or need anything or anyone, do you?' She glances bitterly at the sky. 'Do you?'

The suffering of those who can't love is ignominious, so impure. But since I have come this far already, I will try to see her again in the hospital, as she really was.

The face on the pillow, it is true, has changed very little in a way: the same fineness of bones threatens to break through the fragile-seeming skin. Yet something has drained away. The auburn hair shows a strand of premature grey. Now there is a circumspection, even a meanness, about the mouth. She is no longer beautiful, if she ever was. (Was she?)

I sit beside her. I stare at her in her sleep, but surreptitiously, as if she were naked. Her mouth is half open in a thin-lipped oval of distress, through which the breath whistles in short gasps. The dark crescents of her eyelids, closed now for fifteen hours, join the grey half-moons beneath the eyes to create two voids where the irises should shine – a desert of dying-looking skin, crossed by tiny purple veins. The cruelly plucked eyebrows (she never did let them grow enough) label this mask with a lonely pair of reflex-accents. It is a face no longer even young.

To talk with somebody half emerged from anaesthesia is like talking to a drunk. The barriers are all down. The words come in a passionless whisper. And now her eyelids fly open without warning and the grey eyes are staring at me, but disorientated.

She murmurs: 'Oh Christ. How the hell did you know I was here?' She smiles bleakly. 'Typical of you. The grand romantic gesture. Did you think I was dying?'

Our fingers are meaninglessly entwined. We talk platitudes about her convalescence. She looks down with distaste at her body. Her flippancy (if that is what it was) has gone, and it leaves her almost lifeless.

When I lean forward to hold her shoulders, I am trying to remember my half-love for her.

'Did they have to remove . . . everything?'

'I can't have children, if that's what you mean.'

Yes, she's trembling. I look down at her and try to imagine what that sterility is like. Children, in reality, mean nothing to me: I can't envisage my own. The flesh of her arms is thin and warm in my hands. I can't find anything to say. It is only her own pain that we are momentarily sharing. Then she starts to shake, from deep inside, like the tremors of a motor stopping. 'I always wanted your children.' (Yes, she did say that.) She closes her eyes, as if to blot out the reality of my expression, and turns her head to kiss my fingers. I see her tears falling on to the sheet.

The Small Horse

Steve Walker

The last story in the book is certainly different! Steve Walker is a young poet from Tyneside (in the North of England). Is it a dream? Could there be another country of the small folk, somewhere behind? It is not altogether a new idea. The small people are in old tales. There is Lilliput. There are science fiction stories, too, though here they usually come from some other world. What Steve Walker has done is take the myth out of the books or out of the toy cupboard and place it in what seems to be a rather derelict part of the north-east of England. Or are there other explanations?

I thought it was a mouse at first, and wasn't bothered. Living in a place like this, one must expect the odd mouse. True: it whinnied in the night and woke me up more than once. I climbed out of bed, pulled back the curtains and looked through sleepy eyes at the closed warehouse over the road. I thought the whinnies came from there. True, also: it clip-clopped behind the skirting-board, just like a horse would if horses were small. But I didn't think of that. I took it to be a heavy-footed rodent.

I first saw it one Sunday tea-time – the most miserable time of the week for me; I turn off the TV to avoid the religious programmes and, left with nothing to do, I become miserable: always do. I was buttering some bread when I heard horses' noises. I glanced. Wow! There it was, hoofing the lino by the larder door. A small horse! No larger, indeed, than an underfed mouse – ribs showing, eyes popping. I watched it carefully, stood still with bread in one hand and knife with a scoop of butter on it in the other. Yes, it was certainly, most definitely, a horse, a small horse.

I must say, I've always been the same, ever since I passed twenty. I used to be a songwriter then, or thought I was, but all my songs had been turned down and I was at breaking point. Nothing whatsoever had gone right for me. I'd recently started my present job, and told a salesman I worked with about my problem.

'Give it up,' he jeered at me. 'You've got a good job here. Give it up. You'll never make it.'

What he really meant was: You're an ordinary bloke, like me. You've no business thinking you're a songwriter. People like us aren't songwriters.

He was correct, of course. I followed his advice, but note now that ever since, it seems to me, I've avoided people and things that could be judged as being out of the ordinary. So what was I to do when confronted with the crisis of having a small horse infesting my flat? I needed advice, but only knew ordinary people. I told one or two and they said: 'Come on, man – stop pulling our leg.' And they proceeded to avoid me for the next few days.

I told Mr Ducksbury, my sales-manager. He reacted the same, then started showing me new photos of his grandchildren.

'No. No. Really. I'm serious,' I said.

'Oh, yeah. A small horse? There's no such thing.'

'But there is – I've seen one.'

'Then why's no one else ever seen one? What makes you so special?'

There was a young man who'd worked part-time in the packing department for a bit. I'd avoided talking to him at the time, even when I needed to check on a stock-level, because someone had said he was a painter – oils and all that. I looked up his address in the files. It was near one of my calls – I went there that very day.

'Excuse me.'

'Yes.'

'You may remember me from Hollis's. Can I come in for a moment?'

He let me in.

There were two naked girls seated back to back on a dais thing. He was painting them, all in orange. I was highly embarrassed. One put on a dressing-gown and went to make a pot of tea, but the other just sat there scratching herself. I never got the tea, and didn't gabble through much of my story to the young man, either. He grew sarcastic very quickly and asked me to leave. The girls started laughing as he prodded me out.

When I got back home the horse was drinking from a saucer of milk I'd left out for it. I poured some breakfast cereal into my hand and offered it for the thing to eat. It stood thinking, but wouldn't dare come. I got bored of crouching there, so went off to watch TV.

But I tried to get it to eat from my hand every time I saw it and, at last, a fortnight later, mid-morning – I hadn't bothered to go to work – it trotted up and ate contentedly from my hand. I was thrilled to see it close up. With my feeding, it had put on some weight. What a perfect little thing it was! But, being the way I am, I couldn't tolerate its mystery, its extraordinariness. I decided to kill it, to put poison down and be rid of it.

As soon as this thought entered my mind, the horse gave me a quick look, reared, and galloped away. I pulled off my shoe and threw it after. But my aim was bad; the horse disappeared unharmed through the hole where the plug used to be when I had the old fridge.

A few nights later, I woke up scared. A dream, I thought, already forgotten – or was the horse in my bedroom? I was suddenly petrified of it, as if it were a spider. I searched the bedsheets, looked under the furniture, checked the skirtingboard for cracks, new or old. Nothing. Once again I pulled back the curtains to look at that closed warehouse over the road. I'd always had my suspicions about it, and this time it could be tiny lights shining behind the filthy grilled windows at pavement level.

I got dressed at once, put a torch in my pocket and hurried over. I stood right in front of the grilled windows – but they were too filthy; I couldn't see anything through them.

There was an old door there, on crusty hinges. I kicked it open, two kicks. I switched on my torch and went inside. I was in a foreman's office: cabinets, desk and such still there. A twelve-year-old calendar was on the wall.

I listened. Yes – a mouse-like scratching. This was surely where my small horse had come from, and maybe, I figured, there'd be a whole herd in the warehouse somewhere.

In the light from my torch nothing had any colour. I walked on battered floorboards towards the main storeroom. A tall, wooden sliding door barred my way. I could find no handle and my pushing and coaxing wouldn't budge the thing. I gave it a kick but it was thick and solid and didn't feel it.

What else could I do? I gave up and turned to go. But after only a few steps, I heard the sliding door open behind me. I jumped in fright. Had I pressed a button without realizing it? Was there someone there?

I shone my torch. It flitted across a huge ceiling, showing smashed skylights with the night above. Then I waved it around the warehouse floor.

There were horses, yes, quite a few, just like the one in my flat. But also, everywhere, as if assembled to witness some spectacular event, were people, tiny people. Thousands and thousands of them – all just as tall as a little finger. Most were naked, some wore paper hats and carried spears of broken glass. Lots of them were huddled around little fires they'd made. They stood still in my torchlight, but where my torch couldn't catch, some were running.

I'm home now, in bed with the light on. I'm going to sit up all night reading the Bible out loud.

Acknowledgements

The publishers make grateful acknowledgement to the following for permission to reprint:

'The Poets and the Housewife' by Martin Armstrong, from *The Puppet Show*, copyright © The Estate of Martin Armstrong, and 'Thucydides' by Rachel Gould, copyright © Rachel Gould, 1983, from *Introduction 8* (Faber & Faber 1983), reprinted by permission of A.D. Peters & Co. Ltd. 'Dingo' by F. Bennett, 'The Girl in the Mad Hat' by Dorothy Goulden, 'Trust Mother Audry' by Thomas Hinde and 'The Wedding Jug' by Philip Smith, all from *Twenty Stories*, ed. Francis King, copyright © South East Arts Council, 1985, to Martin Secker & Warburg Ltd. 'The German Boy' by Ron Butlin, copyright © Ron Butlin, 1982, 'The Time Keeper' by Elspeth Davie, copyright © Elspeth Davie, 1978, and 'Three Resolutions to One Kashmiri Encounter' by Giles Gordon, copyright © Giles Gordon, 1981, all from *The Panther Book of Scottish Short Stories* (Grafton Books, 1984), to Collins Publishers Ltd. 'Shopping for One' by Anne Cassidy, copyright © Anne Cassidy, 1984, first published in *Everyday Matters 2: More Short Stories by Women* (Sheba Feminist Publishers, 1984). 'The Curse' by Arthur C. CLarke, from *Reach for Tomorrow* (Gollancz, 1956), which first appeared in *Cosmos*, copyright © Star Publications Inc., 1953, to David Higham Associates and Arthur C. Clarke. Reprinted by permission of the author and the author's agents, Scott Meredith Literary Agency Inc., 845 Third Avenue, New York, NY 10022. 'Getting Used to It' by Douglas Dunn, from *Secret Villages*, copyright © Douglas Dunn, 1985, reprinted by permission of Faber & Faber Ltd. 'Having Taken Off My Wheels' by Martin Elliott, copyright © Martin Elliott, reprinted by permission of the author. 'The Tree House' by Ronald Frame, from *Watching Mrs Gordon and Other Stories* (The Bodley Head), copyright © Ronald Frame, 1983 to the Curtis Brown Group Ltd and the author. 'The Other Launderette' by Helen Harris, copyright © Helen Harris, 1983, from *Introduction 8*, 1983, to Faber & Faber Ltd. 'The Return of the Moon Man' by Eric Malpass, copyright © E. L. Malpass, 1954, reprinted by permission of the author. 'Trotsky's Other Son' by Carol Singh, copyright © Carol Singh, 1985, reprinted by permission of the author. 'Nothing Has Changed' by Colin Thubron, copyright © Colin Thubron, 1985, from *Firebird 4* (Penguin Books, 1985), reprinted by permission of the author. 'The Small Horse' by Steve Walker, copyright © Steve Walker, 1985, to the *Fiction Magazine* and the author.

Although all the stories included in this collection are copyright, it has not proved possible to trace the copyright holders in every case. The publishers would be interested to hear from any not acknowledged here.